MORGAN'S ZOO

Avon Camelot Books by
Deborah and James Howe

BUNNICULA: A RABBIT-TALE OF MYSTERY

Other Avon Camelot Books by
James Howe

THE CELERY STALKS AT MIDNIGHT
HOWLIDAY INN

Avon Flare Books by
James Howe

A NIGHT WITHOUT STARS

JAMES HOWE began his writing career with BUNNICULA, which was published in 1979. This book and the next, TEDDY BEAR'S SCRAP-BOOK, were co-authored with his late wife, Deborah. BUNNICULA went on to receive numerous awards as a favorite among children throughout the U.S. and Canada. It was also made into a popular television special. In 1982, the first "sequel" to BUNNICULA, HOWLIDAY INN, appeared. Prior to that, Howe wrote THE HOSPITAL BOOK, which was nominated for The American Book Award in nonfiction. He is also the author of A NIGHT WITHOUT STARS.

James Howe lives with his wife, Betsy, in Hastings-on-Hudson, New York.

MORGAN'S ZOO

James Howe

Illustrated by
LESLIE MORRILL

AN AVON CAMELOT BOOK

AVON BOOKS
A division of
The Hearst Corporation
1790 Broadway
New York, New York 10019

The Atheneum edition contains the following Library of Congress
Cataloging in Publication Data:

  Howe, James.
  Morgan's zoo.

SUMMARY: When the Chelsea Park Zoo is about to close, Morgan,
the animal keeper, receives help from the animals themselves.
[1. Zoos—Fiction] I. Morrill, Leslie H., ill. II. Title.
PZ7.H83727Mo 1984 [Fic] 84-6325

First Camelot Printing, April 1986

CAMELOT TRADEMARK REG. U. S. PAT. OFF. AND IN
OTHER COUNTRIES, MARCA REGISTRADA, HECHO EN
U. S. A.

Printed in the U.S.A.

OPM 10 9 8 7 6 5 4 3 2 1

To my wife,
Betsy Imershein,
for her many gifts,
not least among them
listening,
laughing,
and wanting to know
what happens next.

Contents

1

There Is No Balloon Man

ON SUNDAY AFTERNOONS the zoo was bustling. Fathers with their sleeves rolled up and jackets draped over their arms bought brightly colored balloons from the balloon man, two for a nickel, and presented them with the admonition to hold them tight to their wide-eyed children. Laughing mothers pointed out the antics of monkeys who gamboled and chattered and who, when they stopped to look out through the bars of their cages, screeched in a way that seemed to small ears to fracture and echo the sound of a mother's laugh. The children dashed ahead, leaving their parents calling out their names, anxious to see once again the Bengal tiger who had so resisted capture, the story was told, that he'd decorated more than one adventurer with stripes to match his own.

For many families, for most families living nearby, a summer without frequent visits to the Chelsea Park Zoo was as unthinkable as a summer without lemonade. It was just something families did together, like bowing their heads for grace before each meal and listening to the radio before they went to bed each night. Oh, it's true that sometimes on a Monday or a Wednesday or a Thursday, the children might put down their stickball bats and run off together to the zoo to become jungle explorers hunting down lions or elephants or crocodiles. Or they might wander by alone on their way home from a piano lesson or a swim in the municipal pool to say hello to their favorite animal, the one who had become their special friend. But for the most part the zoo was a family place, and Sunday afternoon was the family time.

And for the animals . . . well, for the animals, the zoo was a family place, too. They saw themselves and all the people who worked there as one big family. And the people who came to visit them were like relatives gathering together for a Sunday dinner. As with all families, there were certain of those relatives they looked forward to seeing more than others: the ones who slipped them special treats when no one was looking; the ones whose eyes were gentle, whose voices were soft and soothing. And just as the people were sad to have to leave when it grew dark, so the animals were sad to see them go. But everyone was comforted by the thought that there would be another visit soon. And then another. And another. And so on through each long and glorious summer.

BUT THAT WAS all long ago . . . when your mother's mother and your father's father were not even as big as you. The world has changed a great deal in the years since then, not least of all that little corner of it known as the Chelsea Park Zoo. There are still animals, of course, and people come to visit, but not in the numbers they once did. And when they do come, they don't stay long. For a melancholy air, like that of a gray autumn day, pervades the atmosphere. There is no longer a balloon man—there hasn't been for years.

For some, however, the zoo is still a family

place. And if there is a sadness in the air, it is a sweet sadness, comfortable and reassuring in its familiarity. One for whom the zoo is home and its inhabitants the only family he has is a pigeon named William. He was born quite a number of years ago (he himself has lost count) in the eaves above the chimpanzees' cage, about the same time, in fact, that a baby chimpanzee came into the world. William's mother encouraged him to leave his nest, but by the time he was old enough to do so, he had become quite attached to the young chimpanzee and was reluctant to leave him behind. Clarence, for this was the young chimp's name, told William that he must do whatever it was his destiny as a pigeon to do. But William held fast; he was determined to stay close by his friend. And so in time, after William's mother and father and brothers and sisters had all flown away and Clarence's mother and father had been sent to another zoo, Clarence and William found themselves quite alone together. And they were as close as any two brothers could be.

For years, life passed uneventfully at the zoo. That is not to say it was boring, for the animals found much to amuse them in the passage of days and the passing of strangers before their cages. In the evenings, after their visitors had gone home, they whiled away the time telling stories or discussing the day's events. And of course each morning they looked forward to the arrival of their keeper, Morgan.

Morgan had been working at the zoo for as long as anyone could remember. In fact, it was so hard to imagine the zoo *without* Morgan that it had come to be known as Morgan's Zoo. Morgan loved the animals and treated them as if they were all his children, which, since he was a bachelor without any family of his own, they may as well have been. It wasn't long before an animal new to the zoo was won over by his quiet, unassuming manner and the simple fact that he regarded all the animals as his equals. No doubt if you had asked him, Morgan would have said that they *were* his equals for, from what he had seen of mankind, he was quite sure they could be no worse (and wasn't all that convinced they weren't a bit better).

Every morning when Morgan arrived for his day's work (which hardly seemed like work to him), he made the rounds of all the animals' cages, greeting them by name—softly if they were still sleeping or rousing from sleep, heartily if they were awake and awaiting their breakfast. The animals loved this morning ritual; it got the day off to a proper start, reassuring them that all was right with the world. But on *this* morning, this particular morning when our story begins, something changed.

Morgan arrived as usual. But instead of greeting each of the animals, he simply stood before their cages and stared. And sighed. First he stood and stared and sighed before the giraffe's cage. Then he moved on to the lions—Lancelot and Guenevere—and stood and stared and sighed. Unlike Daisy, the giraffe, who had been alarmed by Morgan's behavior, Lancelot did not take too much notice of it. But, of course, these days, Lancelot did not take much notice of anything. He was, as his mate, Guenevere, liked to put it (though only when he was out of hearing), "getting on in years."

Next, Morgan lingered before the seal pool. Basil, the most outgoing of the seals, jumped up out of the water and rested his flippers on the edge of the concrete. Morgan barely noticed. He gazed off into the distance and sighed heavily. Basil, trying to decide whether or not to be insulted by Morgan's seeming indifference, barked loudly. That got Morgan's attention. But his response was not at all what Basil had anticipated. He raised his large hands to his eyes and pulled at the lids as if trying to wipe something away. The wind must have blown some dirt into his eyes, Basil thought, but when he saw a tear wend its way down the byways of Morgan's leathery cheek, he knew something was wrong. He decided not to be insulted. Instead, he was worried.

Clarence and William had been watching all this from Clarence's cage, which was across the way from Daisy and Lance and Gwen and down the path from the seal pool. They didn't know what to make of it, nor did they know what to make of Morgan's behavior when he came to stand before them.

"Oh, Clarence," Morgan sputtered, almost choking on the words before they were out.

Clarence looked out through the bars of his cage with wide, astonished eyes. If William was like a brother to Clarence, Morgan was like a father. And like many children, he did not know what to do when he saw his father in pain and crying. William cocked his head, looking from one to the other. A long silence followed as the animals all stared expectantly at Morgan, wondering what he would do next. Even the elephants who lived next door to Clarence, a mother and daughter known as Lucy and Ginger, had drawn close to the front of their cage, gazing out in amazement.

Suddenly, Morgan gave his shoulders a violent shake and shambled away.

"Do you think I should follow him?" William asked Clarence.

The chimpanzee nodded his head. "That's a good idea," he said. "Maybe you can find out what's going on. Hurry back."

William minced forward through the bars of the cage and lifted himself off and up into the air. As he flew above and away from that part of the zoo he considered his home, he heard the cries of his family below.

"Hurry back!" called Lucy.

"Yes," echoed her daughter, Ginger, "hurry back!"

"We'll be waiting for you, William, old boy," Basil barked.

"Hurry back!" from Gwen, the lioness. And from Lance a low rumble of sound that William took to mean Godspeed.

And as he passed by Daisy's worried eyes, he heard her whisper, "Hurry, William. We've got to help Morgan."

But as William soon learned, it was more than Morgan who needed help.

"STOP BLUBBERING, MAN! It's settled, and that's that. Bawling like a baby isn't going to do you or anybody else any good!"

William was perched outside the window of the zoo's main office. Fortunately, because it was summer, the window was open, which made listening easier. Inside he could see Morgan standing before the desk of Rollo Hackett. While it was true that people thought of Morgan as the zoo's keeper, Hackett was Morgan's boss and therefore the *head* zookeeper—zookeeper in fact but not in spirit. No one liked Rollo Hackett. He was mean and ornery and didn't seem to care much one way or another about any of the animals. Listening to him now as he yelled unsympathetically at Morgan certainly didn't make William like him any better.

Morgan wiped his nose with his crumpled handkerchief and tried to stop crying.

"I can't help myself," he moaned. "It just

doesn't seem fair, that's all. After all these years . . ."

"After all these years, no one gives a hoot about this place anymore, man, can't you see that? Anyway, what are you worried about? You'll be taken care of. The city will find you a job somewhere. And it'll probably be a nice cushy one like—"

"A job?!" Morgan cried in horror. "I don't want a *job!*"

"What do you want?" snarled Rollo Hackett. "Welfare?"

"No, sir, I'm not saying I don't want to work. That's not it at all. It's just that I don't think of my position here as a job. You see, it's the animals I'm thinking of . . . and me . . . it's us I'm thinking of. We're like family, we are, and—"

Hackett's grating laugh made William recoil. " 'Family!' That's a good one. I think it's about time you got away from here, Morgan. You're starting to lose your marbles. They're a bunch of animals, that's all. Nothing more!"

Morgan wiped his nose once more and spoke softly. "Not to me," he said. "Not to me."

"Well," grunted Morgan's boss, "there's

nothing more to talk about. Go on about your business."

"But . . ."

"But nothing!" Hackett exploded. "The zoo is going to be closed down, and that's the end of it. The animals are to be shipped off to other zoos. We're already getting orders for them. Oh, and, by the way . . ."

Morgan looked up at Rollo Hackett. "Yes?" he asked.

"Your pal, the ape, what's his name?"

"Clarence?"

"Yeah, your buddy, Clarence. He's the first to go. We got a zoo in Cincinnati that can't wait to get their hands on him. He's shipping out first thing tomorrow morning."

It would be hard to say who was more dumbfounded by this particular piece of news, Morgan or William. William stood frozen to the spot as he listened to Morgan struggle for words to express his anguish.

"There . . . there must be some mistake," Morgan stammered. "Not . . . Clarence. Not . . . tomorrow. It can't be. Please, Mr. Hackett. You don't understand. Clarence is like a—"

"Like a what?" Hackett said with a sneer.

"Like a son, I suppose. Well, then, the sooner we separate you two the better. It's an unhealthy attachment, if you ask me. Now, didn't you have something you needed to do?" And he went back to the papers lying on his desk while ignoring the man with stooped shoulders who stood empty and depleted before him.

William watched Morgan stuff his much-used handkerchief back into his pocket and turn to go out the door.

He felt almost dizzy as he tried to make sense of everything he'd just heard. The zoo was to be closed. Morgan and all the animals sent away. And Clarence was to be shipped off tomorrow! His home, his family, his very best friend . . . all wiped away in a moment because . . . because . . . just because. He realized he didn't know why this was happening. He vowed to find out. But he knew what he had to do first. He must return to his waiting friends and tell them all what fate held in store for them.

As he glided high above the zoo, he saw Morgan trudging along beneath him, bearing the weight of the food buckets he carried much as William bore the heaviness of his own heart. He saw in the distance the animals awaiting him.

They stood stock-still, staring up at him, watching him rise and fall on the currents of air as he made his way closer and closer to them. For a moment he imagined he saw the cages and the pool empty, their inhabitants gone and forgotten. He imagined he heard a silence so still it deafened him. He imagined he saw himself alone, picking at the ground and finding nothing there.

He blinked and saw that his friends were still there in the distance. They grew closer and closer until he coasted down for a landing on the edge of Clarence's cage. All eyes were on him. Everyone was waiting. Waiting for him to speak.

2

Allison and Andrew

"THE ZOO is going to be *closed.*"

The words tumbled from his mouth so abruptly and were greeted by such a silence that for a moment William wondered if he had spoken at all. Everywhere he looked he saw the same raised brows, the same astounded eyes, the same slack jaws. His head bobbed nervously as he waited for a response.

At last, Basil broke the silence.

"Are you sure, William?" he said in an uncharacteristically soft voice. "I mean to say, are you quite sure?"

William glanced at Clarence, whose face was sad and bewildered. "Quite sure," he said. "I heard Rollo Hackett tell Morgan that the zoo was to be closed down, and all the animals—"

"Oh, dear, what about all the animals?" cried Gwen.

"Yes, what's to become of us?" Lucy asked in a hushed voice, as if she thought she could hide her alarm from her daughter.

William turned his gaze away from Clarence's face, finding it hard to bear the sadness he saw there.

"All of you," he said with a catch in his throat, "are to be sent to other zoos to live."

"Other zoos!" Daisy cried.

"It can't be," said Gwen.

Lance, who was a little hard-of-hearing, turned to his mate. "What's that?" he asked. "What's all the fuss and bother about?"

"It's the zoo," she replied loudly. "They're going to close the zoo and send us all away."

"I hope they're not sending us back to the jungle," replied Lance gruffly. "I lost my taste for antelope a long time ago."

"They're not sending anyone to the jungle," William assured Lance. "You're going to other zoos."

"When?" asked Daisy. "When is all this supposed to happen?"

William made sure he kept his eyes from meeting Clarence's as he uttered his next words. "Well," he said slowly, "I'm not sure about *everyone*, but I know that Clarence is . . . supposed to be leaving . . . tomorrow." He said "tomorrow" so softly that no one heard.

"What's that?" asked Basil.

"When?" Daisy inquired.

"I didn't hear," said Clarence. "When am I leaving?"

William felt his eyes sting as he cocked his head and looked up at Clarence. "Tomorrow," he repeated a little louder. "There's a zoo in Cincinnati . . ." and he trailed off and could say no more.

"Tomorrow," Clarence said in a shocked whisper. He slumped against the bars of his cage, sank to the ground, and scratched his head. William had never seen his friend look so confused, so defeated. In the past when there was any sort of trouble, Clarence was always the first to say, "Look on the bright side." That and "Where there's a will, there's a way" were two of Clarence's favorite expressions. But one look into Clarence's woebegone eyes would tell you that, for him, the "bright side" had vanished with William's pronouncement.

Just then, Morgan arrived, food buckets clattering, and the animals watched in silence as he went from cage to cage, unlocking doors, filling troughs, clanging doors shut. Morgan barely looked at them, and they, appetites gone, scarcely touched their breakfasts.

Clarence clung to the bars of his cage, pressing himself against them, his eyes searching Morgan's face for an answer, or at least for some hope. But Morgan could give him neither. His own eyes were rimmed with red, and when he spoke his voice crackled.

"Good morning, Clarence," he said, as if he'd not seen Clarence—or any of the other animals, for that matter—just twenty minutes before. "How are you this morning?" He opened Clarence's door and placed some scraps in his food trough. "Hope you're hungry," Morgan went on. "I've got some nice oranges here and some bread and . . ."

Clarence let go of the bars and ran across the cage to grab hold of Morgan's leg. He held on to him with all his strength, which, since he was a chimpanzee, was considerable. Morgan reached down and stroked Clarence's head. "I can't put anything over on you, can I?" he said softly. "*You* know something's up." And then he sighed. "Oh, Clarence, what are we going to do, hmm?"

"Hi, Morgan!"

Morgan looked up to see the twins standing before Clarence's cage. It was Andrew who had spoken. It usually was Andrew who spoke first since his sister was the quieter of the two. In fact, it often surprised people to be told that Andrew and Allison were twins at all because not only their looks but their personalities were as different as could be.

"What's the matter with Clarence?" Andrew went on. "Is he sick or something?"

"Sick?" Morgan replied. "No, not really. It's just that we've had some bad news here today, and—"

"What happened?" cried Andrew.

Without realizing it, Morgan placed his hands over Clarence's ears. "They're closing the zoo," he said in a false whisper. "And they're sending Clarence off to Cincinnati first thing tomorrow morning." Clarence tightened his grasp of Morgan's leg.

"They can't do that!" Andrew said defiantly. Andrew was eleven, and he believed firmly that saying things made them so. But Morgan was much older than eleven, and he knew otherwise.

"I'm afraid they can," he said. "There's nothing I can do about it. After all, it isn't my zoo."

"It isn't?" Allison's voice registered surprise. She had never called the Chelsea Park Zoo anything but Morgan's Zoo, so she didn't understand what Morgan was talking about. "Can't you just tell them you don't want them to close the zoo?" she asked.

Morgan smiled for the first time that day. "I wish it were that simple," he said.

"What we need is a plan!" Andrew announced.

Morgan sat down on a tree stump that had been placed in Clarence's cage long ago and pulled Clarence up onto his lap. "A plan," he mused.

"Sure," Andrew went on, full of determination. "We've got to figure out a way to save the zoo."

"That's a pretty tall order," Morgan said, shaking his head. In truth, much as Morgan liked

Andrew and Allison, he didn't have much faith that they'd come up with a way to save the zoo. But Andrew's suggestion did get him to thinking that perhaps there *was* something to be done. Perhaps he didn't have to just sit back and let the inevitable happen. A moment ago, he had smiled for the first time; now for the first time he felt hope.

A scowl crossed Andrew's face as if he were deep in thought. "Let's see," he said, "we can't just save the zoo like *that!*" And he snapped his fingers. "We have to take it a step at a time. First, we have to make sure they don't send Clarence to Cincinnati . . . I've got it!" Andrew's face lit up with the certainty that he'd found the answer.

All the animals peered out through the bars of their cages, hopeful that the key to their redemption would lie in the next words Andrew would utter. Morgan was not so hopeful. He couldn't believe anyone, even Andrew, bright as he was, could come up with a solution that quickly.

"Call Cincinnati and tell them that Clarence just died!" said Andrew grandly.

"Died!" cried Morgan in alarm, hugging Clarence to him. The animals were aghast.

"Andrew," said Allison. "That's a terrible idea. How can you even say such a thing?"

"Boy," Andrew said, "I'm not saying he really died or anything. I'm saying you tell *them* that. Then they'll forget all about him, and you won't have to send him away."

Morgan thought it over for a minute.

"I'd never get away with it," he said at last. "Mr. Hackett would be sure to find out. And then he'd just call the zoo in Cincinnati right back and tell them Clarence was alive and well and all theirs. I'm sorry, Andrew, but we'll have to come up with a better idea. Maybe it would help if we walked while we thought. After all, Clarence and I haven't had our morning constitutional yet."

And so Morgan and Clarence and Andrew and Allison walked slowly down the path that led them in the direction of the aviary. William followed along, flying then walking, walking then flying, trying to hear what he could of their deliberations.

For a time there was nothing to hear but the sound of footsteps. Everyone seemed lost in thought. No doubt Morgan and Clarence were wondering if this morning's constitutional would be their last. They had gone for walks together

every morning after breakfast for as long as either of them could remember. Usually, they went alone, but on occasion Allison and Andrew joined them.

Perhaps Allison and Andrew were thinking about the wonderful summer they'd been having with Morgan and the animals. Though their parents had decided they would be going away to camp this year, the arrangements had never been made, what with the confusion of their father's moving out and the divorce and all. And then their mother had grown so busy with her job that she'd forgotten all about it until it was too late. They'd been just as happy not to go, but had found that with most of their friends away they'd had many long hours to fill. And so, since they lived nearby, they'd begun spending much of their time in the park.

One early summer day, they'd spotted Morgan eating his lunch alone on a bench. They asked if they could join him, and in no time at all were asking him question after question about life at the zoo. If they were so interested, he said, why didn't they come back with him and see for themselves what went on there? They did, and soon they were coming everyday. They got to know all the animals and, best of all, to help Morgan with his chores. Even though their friends would soon be returning home and school would be starting, they intended to continue coming to the zoo as often as they could. That is, if there was any longer a zoo to come to.

"I know!" said Andrew suddenly. "We'll tell the zoo in Cincinnati that Clarence disappeared."

"That's almost as bad as your first idea," Allison commented.

"I'm afraid I'm inclined to agree with Allison," said Morgan. "After all, we're still faced with the same problem. Mr. Hackett will find out and just call them back."

Andrew drew his lips tightly together. "I guess you're right," he said unhappily.

Just then, Allison had a thought. "Morgan," she said, "what if Clarence *did* disappear?"

"What do you mean?" Morgan wanted to know.

"Well," she went on calmly, "if there was some way we could hide him for a while—"

"Right," said Andrew, picking up the idea. "You could tell Mr. Hackett that Clarence ran away or something. Maybe we could take him home with us."

"Sure, Andrew," Allison said. "And what do you think Mom will say about it?"

"Oh, yeah. Mom."

"But," said Allison, her face bright with a new idea, "what if *you* took him home, Morgan? You live by yourself, don't you?"

Morgan rubbed his head. "Well, I don't know," he said slowly. "I *do* live alone, it's true. But I have a landlady, Miss Twillery, and I don't think she'd cotton to the idea. We're not allowed to have pets, you see."

"Too bad," Allison said with a sigh. Clarence reached out and squeezed her hand. Allison felt sure he'd understood everything they'd been talking about.

"I would never think of Clarence as a 'pet,' " said Allison. "He's just like one of us."

At that, Andrew stopped dead in his tracks. "That's it!" he shouted.

William, who had been trailing behind the others, flew to catch up when he heard Andrew's sudden cry.

"What's 'it'?" Allison asked.

"What you just said—that Clarence is like one of us," replied Andrew. "If we put some clothes on him, Morgan could take him home and tell his landlady Clarence is his nephew or something. He could say . . . let's see . . . he could say he's come to visit for a few days from . . . from . . . Cincinnati!"

Morgan looked doubtful. But then he remembered something that made him ask himself if it just might not work.

"Miss Twillery," he said slowly, "is very nearsighted. She can barely see two feet in front of her without her glasses, *which* . . ." he paused for emphasis ". . . she is too vain to wear."

"In other words," Andrew said, "it's just possible she might not be able to tell the difference between Clarence the chimpanzee and Clarence—"

Morgan finished the sentence for him. "—my nephew from Cincinnati! I'll do it!" Morgan cried. "I've never done such a crazy thing in my life, but to save Clarence, I'd do anything."

Morgan pulled Clarence up into his arms. "So, nephew," he said, "what do you say we find you some clothes?"

3

Morgan's "Nephew"

WHEN THE TAXI DRIVER glanced into his rearview mirror, his cigar almost fell out of his mouth.

"Where ya headed, Mac?" he asked Morgan. "The circus?"

Morgan tried to remain calm. He was still not convinced that this little scheme the twins had cooked up was going to work at all. Clarence sat at his side, neatly dressed in a shirt, tie, pants held up by suspenders, an old pair of running shoes, and a large hat Morgan hoped would help disguise his true identity. So far it didn't seem to be working.

"No," he said to the driver. Then, giving his address, he added, "This is my nephew. He's come to visit me."

At that, the driver jerked round in his seat. He stared at Clarence, then at Morgan, and then shook his head. "Well, for your sake," he said at last, "I hope whatever he's got don't run in the family."

Morgan breathed deeply as the taxi pulled away from the curb to carry him and his "nephew" home. It had been a long day, and he would be glad when it was over. One hope he nurtured: that Miss Twillery would not be sitting out front on the porch, as was her custom on summer afternoons. Perhaps, because he had waited till the dinner hour, she would be in her kitchen, and he would escape her notice.

But as the taxi pulled up before the house, he saw at once that such good fortune was not to be his. There she sat as always, doggedly rocking and just as doggedly fanning away the summer heat. Nervously, Morgan paid the driver and opened the door of the taxi.

"Now, Clarence," he whispered as he took

his charge's hand, "try to behave as much like a little boy as you know how. Just think about Andrew and do what he would do." In his other hand, Morgan carried the valise that Allison had been smart enough to think of.

"After all," she'd told Morgan and Andrew, "we can't have Morgan arrive with his nephew and no suitcase. What would Miss Twillery say?"

What Miss Twillery *did* say was, "Good evening, Morgan. My, aren't you working late today?"

"Evening, Miss Twillery," replied Morgan casually, as if arriving home with a chimpanzee on his arm was something he did every night. "I'm late," he went on, "because I had to pick up my nephew at the train station. He's come in from Cincinnati to pay me a visit."

"Well, isn't that nice?" said Miss Twillery. She stopped rocking then and leaned forward, squinting fiercely. The bun of blonde hair that she wore atop her head (which Morgan suspected wasn't nature's gift) toppled forward slightly. She gave it a shove with her hand as she smiled at the figure standing next to Morgan.

"Hello, young man," she said in a syrupy voice. "And what is *your* name?" Miss Twillery

had a way of speaking to children that, were Clarence really a child, would have made him want to kick her.

"His name is Tommy," Morgan said quickly.

"Tommy," cooed Miss Twillery. "Isn't that a *nice* name? And how old are you, Tommy, dear?"

"He's seven," replied Morgan.

Miss Twillery extended her hand. "How do you do, Tommy?" she said.

Clarence understood the meaning of her gesture and reached out to place his hand in hers accordingly.

Miss Twillery gasped. "Oh, my! What a large hand for such a small child."

Feeling beads of sweat form on his brow, Morgan stammered, "It's . . . that is . . . he's . . . he's wearing a baseball mitt."

"Ah," said Miss Twillery, releasing Clarence's hand. "Well, I suppose boys will be boys. Still, he's an awfully quiet one, isn't he?"

"He's shy," Morgan said. In an effort to look the part, Clarence hung his head and dragged his sneakered toe back and forth across the floor.

"Well, *I* was shy when I was his age," Miss Twillery said simperingly. "I certainly know how he feels." She leaned toward Clarence and looked deeply into his eyes. "Tommy, you and I shall have to spend some time together," she said. "Then you won't feel so shy."

Morgan was frantically trying to think of a response when Miss Twillery turned to face him. "Why, Morgan," she said. "I've just noticed something about Tommy I hadn't seen before."

"What's that?" Morgan asked nervously. He was sure the game was up.

"He looks just like you. How silly of me not to have seen the family resemblance at once."

Morgan stifled a chuckle. "People say that all the time," he managed to get out. And then he felt such relief that he could no longer contain himself. Laughter rippled from him, catching Miss Twillery in its waves. Soon she too was laughing, though she was not altogether sure why.

Clarence watched with amusement and before he was aware of it, he too began to laugh. Now the sound of a chimpanzee laughing is not the same as the sound of a person laughing. And Miss Twillery, nearsighted as she was, was *not* hard of hearing.

"What a *peculiar* laugh Tommy has!" she said, catching her breath.

Morgan, panicking, started to make sounds as close to Clarence's as he could manage.

"Morgan!" cried Miss Twillery. "Whatever has overtaken you?"

Clarence, realizing he'd made a blunder, brought his laughter quickly under control. Relieved, Morgan followed suit. "Oh," he said breathlessly, "it's nothing. It's just the way we laugh in our family. A family trait, you might say."

If Miss Twillery doubted what Morgan was telling her, she didn't show it. "I see," she said, nodding slowly. "Well, I always say there's no telling about families."

"How true," Morgan agreed. "Well, I think perhaps we'd better go inside and freshen up. Goodnight, Miss Twillery."

"Goodnight, Morgan. And, Tommy, I hope I'll be seeing lots more of you."

"Oh, I doubt it," said Morgan hastily. He pushed Clarence through the open door into the house. "I mean . . . I expect I'll be keeping him very busy sightseeing and all."

"Well, of course," said Miss Twillery

sweetly. "And don't forget to take him to the zoo."

"The zoo," said Morgan, easing his way inside. "I'll be sure to remember."

Once inside his room, Morgan collapsed against the locked door. "Whew," he said to Clarence, who was testing out the bed, "we did it. We actually got away with it. I can't believe it." He dropped the empty suitcase to the floor and sat down next to Clarence. "So far, so good," he said. "Now, I just have to deal with Mr. Hackett."

"HE WHAT?" Rollo Hackett shouted the next day.

"He escaped, sir," Morgan replied meekly. "I don't know how it happened. I went to his cage this morning and—"

"Don't know how it *happened!* Don't tell me you don't know how it happened. That ape is supposed to ship out of here *this* morning! Now where is he?"

"I'm telling you I don't know, Mr. Hackett. I arrived for work this morning, and his cage was empty. It's all my fault, I'm sure. I must have left the lock undone. Otherwise, there's no way he could have—"

Rollo Hackett slammed his fist down on his

desk. "I want you to find him, Morgan!" he demanded. "I don't care how you do it or where you have to look, but I want that monkey found pronto, you get my drift?"

Morgan lifted the cap he'd been holding in his hands and placed it on his head. He almost felt he should salute. "Yes, sir," he replied. "I'll do my best to locate him, sir."

"You do that, Morgan," Hackett growled. "Leave no banana peel unturned, understand? And Morgan—"

"Yes, Mr. Hackett?"

"I don't want anybody finding out about this. I'll stall Cincinnati somehow. But mum's the word, got it?"

"You bet, Mr. Hackett. Mum's the word."

When Morgan saw Allison and Andrew later that morning, he almost jumped for joy.

"It's working!" he exclaimed excitedly. "Miss Twillery believed Clarence was my nephew. And I think Mr. Hackett bought the escape story. I don't know how long we can keep it going, but at least it's given us some time to think what to do next."

"I have an idea," said Allison in her soft voice.

"What is it?" Morgan asked.

"Why don't we write the President?"

Andrew snickered. "Boy, you tell me *I* have dumb ideas," he said. "That's the dumbest one I ever heard."

"The President *likes* animals," Allison protested. "Don't you remember when he was trying to be elected, there were pictures of elephants and donkeys everywhere?"

Andrew slapped his forehead with the palm of his hand. "That doesn't mean anything," he said. "Those are symbols for the Democrats and Republicans."

"Oh, yeah."

"Wait a minute," said Morgan, who had been thinking all this time. "Allison has given me an idea of something we *can* do."

"See?" said Allison. "Morgan thinks we should write the President, too."

"No, Allison," Morgan said. "I don't know that that would do us much good. But I could go talk with the Mayor. After all, it was his decision to close the zoo. He seems like a decent sort of person. Maybe he'd listen to me. Anyway, it's worth a try."

"It sure is," Andrew agreed.

"I'll say," said Allison. "Could you talk to him today?"

"Yes," said Morgan staunchly. "We have no time to lose. I'll go down to his office first thing this afternoon. I'll demand to see him. After all, I'm a citizen—and this is an emergency!"

"Yay, Morgan!" cried the twins. They felt certain that once the Mayor had heard Morgan's plea, the zoo would be saved.

William, who had been standing nearby during this conversation, overheard Morgan's plan. He decided immediately that he, too, would visit City Hall. After all, the other animals were depending on him for news and the kind of leadership they had come to rely on in Clarence. With Clarence temporarily out of the picture, William knew a lot rested on his shoulders. But he was inspired by Morgan's determination. And he wondered: might *he* play a part in saving the zoo? Was it possible to be an ordinary pigeon one day and a hero the next?

It was not long before he saw Morgan departing for City Hall. "Goodbye, everyone," he cried out to his friends as he flew off in the zoo-keeper's shadow. "I'm off to see the Mayor. Wish me luck!"

"Wish me luck!" Morgan called back to Allison and Andrew, who were standing by the seal pool, waving.

"Good luck, Morgan!" they shouted.

"Good luck, William!" cried the animals.

And so Morgan and William set off on their quest.

4

William Takes Wing

MAYOR THAYER was a bald-headed man with a gently sloping paunch that evidenced his love of fine food. Aside from his reputation as a gourmand, he was known to be a politician who cared about his constituents and wanted nothing more than to please them. However, recent pressures from the City Council had necessitated his making a number of severe cuts in the city's budget. As a result, his popularity among the people was in decline. Depressed over this, he had taken to hiding away in his office and eating nothing but junk food.

When Morgan arrived at City Hall, Mayor

Mayor Thayer regarded Morgan sympathetically. If ever there was a man who seemed more miserably unhappy than he himself, it was Morgan. Perhaps, just perhaps, he might be able to do something to make him happy. After all, he reasoned, one happy citizen was better than none. It was worth a try.

"Come in," said Mayor Thayer. Morgan stepped quickly into the Mayor's office. "And Bernice," the Mayor said, turning back to his secretary.

"Yes?"

"Don't forget the pickles."

Fortunately, the time it had taken Morgan to get in to see the Mayor, together with the lack of air-conditioning, worked to William's advantage. For he was now perched on the ledge of the open window right outside the Mayor's office. It had taken him some time to find the window he was looking for, and then he'd had to negotiate a place for himself to stand. This was no small accomplishment since, as everyone knows, the window ledges of municipal office buildings are popular spots among pigeons. Now, he was quite settled in and ready to hear what the Mayor had to say.

"It's about the zoo," Morgan began. "I work there, you see, and I've heard that the zoo is to be closed. I was hoping—"

"Oh, dear," said the Mayor, "I did so want to make you happy. But if it's about the zoo, there's really nothing to be done."

"But *why?*" protested Morgan. "Think of all the pleasure it gives people. Why, everyone loves a zoo!"

"I'm afraid they don't," the Mayor replied. "That's just the problem. Fewer and fewer people visit the zoo every year. They think the park is unsafe—"

Morgan shot forward in his chair. "But it isn't!" he cried.

"Well, you and I may know that, but people are afraid. They hear about all sorts of crimes in the city, and they just stay away from places where there aren't a lot of people."

"But couldn't you put more policemen in the park?"

"I'd like to," said Mayor Thayer with a sigh, "but we just don't have the money. You see, that's the other part of the problem. We have to cut down on expenses. And the zoo has become a financial drain on the city. I'm sorry, Mr.—"

"Morgan."

"Mr. Morgan, but my hands are tied. Believe me, I have nothing against animals, but—"

"What's to become of them?" Morgan asked plaintively. "Are they really to be sent off to other zoos around the country? Are they to be separated from each other, the only family they've ever known?"

The Mayor stared down at his hands, which were folded on his desk. Morgan could see from the whiteness of his knuckles that this conversation was not an easy one for him. "I'm sorry," Mayor Thayer said. "Really I am." He looked up at Morgan and attempted a smile. "I'm sure it will all work out for the best. The animals will be sent to homes where they're really wanted, where people will come and see them every day. And soon they'll make new friends and forget all about each other." He knew he didn't really believe this, but what else could he say?

"As for you and Mr. Hackett," he went on, "why, you'll be well taken care of. We'll find you good jobs in the Parks Department. In fact, I believe Mr. Hackett is in line for a big promotion. You'll see—everything will work out for the best."

He reached across his desk then and picked up a waxed bag lying on some papers. "Care for a donut?" he asked Morgan, extending the bag toward him.

Morgan stood. "No, thank you," he replied. "I came here for hope, Mr. Mayor, not donuts."

"I'm sorry," Mayor Thayer said a little wistfully, "but donuts are all I have to offer."

Morgan turned toward the door, then turned back.

"Just one last question," he said. "When is the zoo scheduled to be closed?"

"Two weeks from today," came the Mayor's reply.

Morgan felt as though someone had punched him in the stomach. "Two weeks," he repeated to himself. "Two weeks."

Because Morgan left the Mayor's office in something of a daze, he did not return immediately to the zoo. Instead, he wandered the streets trying to figure out what possible solution there might be to a situation that seemed completely beyond his control.

William, however, barely waited for the Mayor to finish his pronouncement before taking flight and returning home.

"Two weeks!" he shouted as he landed on the edge of the seal pool. Basil, glistening in the afternoon sun, pulled himself up on his flippers.

"What's that?" he asked. "What about two weeks?"

"That's when the zoo's going to close," said William. "In two weeks!" Murmurs rushed like wildfire round the animals' cages. William went on to report everything he'd overheard at the Mayor's office, and when he finished, silence, like a sudden fog, filled the air.

"Well, I guess that's it," growled Lance. "I mean, if the Mayor says we're going to close up shop, well, then, we're going to close up shop. There's nothing anybody can do about it."

Lucy sighed. "Ah, my dear, dear friends," she proclaimed rather dramatically. "To think that we shall soon be parted. I will never forget you, I promise you that. You shall always have a place in my heart." It should be noted here that Lucy was once a circus elephant—the star of the show, as she often reminded others—and as a result was prone to show business mannerisms that amused some, annoyed others, and deeply embarrassed her daughter, Ginger.

"Oh, Mother," Ginger said. "We're not leaving *yet!*"

"Well, I know, dear," replied Lucy. "But I wanted everyone to know how I feel."

"Lucy," said Daisy from across the way, "we all know how you feel. It's how we all feel. None of us wants to leave here. And if we do have to leave—"

"Yes," Gwen said, finishing her best friend's sentence, as she often did, "*if* we do, we'll *all* miss each other."

"What are you two saying 'if' for?" said Lance. "We're leaving, aren't we? That much is clear."

"You're right, dear," said Gwen. "We're leaving. And so soon, too. Oh, William, I had so hoped you would bring us some word of encouragement from the Mayor."

"So did I," William said. "But he seemed as unhappy about it as we are."

"Hmph," snorted Basil. "I doubt that. After all, *he's* not being forced to leave his home and family."

Lucy began to sniff. "It's so sad," she said. "I don't believe I've felt this atrabilious since I was retired—prematurely, I might add—from the circus."

Everyone nodded sympathetically. No one bothered to ask Lucy what "atrabilious" meant since she was always using big words like that and rarely knew their meaning. Ginger looked around at all the long faces and suddenly grew quite angry.

"Look at you," she said sharply. "Just like a bunch of grown-ups!"

"Well, that's what we are, dear," said her mother.

"But you've all given up!" she declared. "We have *two* whole weeks to think of a way out of this. But you don't even want to try!"

"Ginger, dear, you're a positive inspiration," remarked Daisy. There was a lilt in her voice that hadn't been there before. "A breath of fresh air. Yes, we must put on our thinking-caps and see if indeed there isn't something we can do."

"But what?" asked Gwen. "The whole thing seems like a . . . a . . ."

"A *fait accompli!*" said Lucy. "I agree. There's nothing any of *us* can do."

"I doubt that Clarence would agree with you if he were here," Basil remarked.

"You're right, Basil," said Daisy. "Clarence would know what to do. Why don't we—"

"—ask Clarence," Gwen said. "What a wonderful idea. William, you must fly at once to Morgan's house and consult with Clarence. Do you know the way?"

"Yes," said William. "I've followed Morgan home sometimes. I'm sure I could find my way alone."

"Then off with you, William," said Basil with some urgency. "Let's find out what Clarence has to say on the subject. After all, he's the smart one around here. And now that he doesn't have to worry about saving his own skin—at least for the time being—he's probably already given the matter some thought. Well, William, what're you waiting for? Off you go!"

And so for the second time that day William found himself off on a mission of great importance.

WHEN HE ARRIVED at Miss Twillery's boarding house, he did not see a soul stirring. The day had turned uncomfortably hot and sticky, and so, William concluded, whoever was at home was undoubtedly sitting inside the shaded rooms in front of whirring fans trying to keep cool. But when he flew up to Morgan's room he was in for something of a surprise.

The window was wide open, and Clarence was nowhere in sight.

"Clarence! Clarence!" William called out. But there was no reply. "Clarence, where are you?" Sunlight flooded the sparsely furnished room; it would have been difficult to miss seeing a chimpanzee if indeed a chimpanzee were there to be seen. William wondered: might Clarence have run away? Quickly, he flew from the windowsill to the backyard.

There, he spotted the landlady, Miss Twillery, and another woman seated in lawn chairs sipping lemonade. No sooner had he seen them than the second woman turned and looked in his direction. Her glass slipped from her hand as she jumped up and screamed. William could not believe that the sight of an ordinary pigeon could be quite that alarming. But then he realized that she was staring and pointing at something behind him.

"What is it, Evelyn?" cried Miss Twillery. "For heaven's sake, what's the matter with you?"

"Hilda!" Evelyn shrieked. "There's a chimp in your chestnut!"

At that, both Miss Twillery and William

turned sharply and looked behind them. There swinging through the branches of the tree that towered beside the house was Clarence, blissfully unaware of the commotion he was causing.

"Clarence!" William called, aghast.

Clarence turned suddenly at hearing his name being called.

"Clarence!" William said again. "Go back to Morgan's room. Hurry!"

Bewildered, Clarence clambered up through the tree and through the open window.

"He's gone into the house!" screamed Evelyn. She carried on so that one swing of her arm caught the pitcher of lemonade and toppled it from the table onto her foot. "What's that!" she cried.

"For goodness' sake, Evelyn, do calm down! It's just the lemonade. Now we must think what to do."

"Well, if it were up to *me*," said Evelyn, "I'd call the police."

"Nonsense," replied Miss Twillery. "I'll call Morgan. He knows about animals. He'll tell us what to do. Oh, thank heavens his dear little nephew wasn't here to see this! I'm sure it would have scared the poor lad out of his wits." Miss

Twillery proceeded into the house, followed by the quite hysterical Evelyn.

William, meanwhile, had followed Clarence into Morgan's room and was trying hard to understand how what he had just witnessed had come to be.

"It's so unlike you to take such chances," said William, trying hard not to lecture his old friend, or sound like a parent. "Why couldn't you just stay in the room the way you were supposed to?"

"I don't know what got into me," Clarence said, shaking his head. "It was so hot and stuffy in here. I opened the window to get some fresh air, and then I spotted that beautiful tree outside. The sun was shining and a little breeze was stirring. Do you have any idea how much I've longed to swing through a big tree like that all my life, William? You've been free to come and go from the time you were born. But I've always lived in a cage. And even though I go out from time to time for walks with Morgan, that's just not the same as *freedom*. I thought . . . I thought just this once, I would know what it's like to swing freely through the air, to be confined by nothing . . . nothing at all."

"Oh, Clarence," said William, "I understand.

At least, I think I do. But look at the price you've paid. Now you've been seen. Who knows what Miss Twillery will do? Maybe you *should* run away, Clarence—*really* run away, I mean."

Clarence shook his head. "No," he replied. "That would just get Morgan into more trouble. I'd better stay put and take whatever's coming to me."

Down in the kitchen, Miss Twillery listened as the telephone rang on the other end of the line.

Evelyn was standing at the sink drinking a bicarbonate of soda. "My stomach's in an absolute tizzy," she said breathlessly. "Why, I never thought I'd live to see the day a wild animal would be rampaging through my own neighborhood. A gorilla, no less!"

"I thought you said it was a chimpanzee," Miss Twillery replied.

"Well, it was an awfully *big* chimpanzee if that's what it was, I'll tell you—"

"Sshh!" said Miss Twillery suddenly. Someone had answered on the other end. "Is this the zoo?" she asked.

"Yeah," said Rollo Hackett irritably.

"Is Morgan there?" Miss Twillery inquired.

"Nope, I haven't seen him. What'd ya want?"

"Well, I had hoped to speak to Morgan, but I may as well tell you. I am Morgan's landlady, and I believe I have just spotted an ape of some sort swinging through my tree."

Rollo Hackett jerked his feet off his desk and sat up suddenly. "What's that you say?" he asked. "What kind?"

"Chestnut," replied Miss Twillery.

"Not the tree, lady," snapped Mr. Hackett. "What kind of ape?"

"Oh. Well, my friend here says she believes it is a chimpanzee—"

"Gorilla," Evelyn interjected.

"A *large* chimpanzee."

"A large chimpanzee," Rollo Hackett repeated, a grin growing across his face. Just then, Morgan walked into the office.

"Don't you worry, lady," said Hackett. "I'll send a man right over to pick him up. And I've got *just* the man for the job."

"Thank you," said Miss Twillery. "My address is—"

"You don't have to give me the address. The man I'm sending won't have any trouble finding the place."

After Rollo Hackett had put down the receiver, he looked up at Morgan. "I've got a little job for you, Morgan," he said. As he spoke, he cracked his knuckles—slowly, one at a time.

"Yes, sir?" asked Morgan.

"It seems there's an animal on the loose. Sounds surprisingly like our little lost friend. And you'll never guess where he's been spotted, Morgan."

Morgan felt his face turn red. "Where?" he asked. His heart was beating rapidly.

"Oh, come on," said Rollo Hackett. "*Guess.*"

"I . . . I really don't know," said Morgan, stammering.

"Why, Morgan, a bright person like yourself and you can't come up with one little guess? Well, then, let me put it to you this way: I want you to go home—that's right, to the house where you live—and I believe you'll find there one missing chimp. How he got there I can't imagine. And frankly, I don't want to know. The important thing is that he's been found. Now, I want you over there pronto to pick him up, got it?"

"Yes, sir," said Morgan meekly. "I'll pick him up right away, Mr. Hackett."

"You do that little thing," snarled Rollo

Hackett. "And meanwhile, I'll call that zoo in Cincinnati and tell them the good news. He may be arriving a day late, but they've got their chimp!"

5

Another Plan

MORGAN WAS SURE that this was the worst day of his life. First, he had had his disappointing interview with Mayor Thayer. Now, he and Clarence had been found out and, within hours, would be separated. As the Number 10 bus carried him home, he couldn't help but recall the thinly disguised glee with which Rollo Hackett had informed him of Clarence's discovery and ordered him to bring him back. Why did his boss take such pleasure from rubbing salt in his wounds? Mr. Hackett was certainly the most disagreeable person Morgan had ever known, but he didn't hate him for it. He could only feel pity for a man so empty he had nothing, not even a pinch of compassion, to give to others.

As the day turned out, however, it was far from the worst in Morgan's life. For when he and Clarence returned to Rollo Hackett's office, reconciled to their imminent parting, they were met with a great and wonderful surprise.

"He's not going," Rollo Hackett mumbled bitterly as Morgan and Clarence appeared at the door.

"What?" asked Morgan in disbelief.

"You heard me," Hackett grumbled. "He's not going. Just put 'im back in his cage."

"But . . ."

Rollo Hackett, puffy and red-faced from the exertion of having to tell someone good news, pounded his fist on the desk. "This is all *your* fault, Morgan!" he snapped. "If it hadn't been for you and your monkeyshines, that ape would be on his way to Cincinnati."

"What happened?" Morgan asked, barely able to contain his joy.

"What do you think happened? They found another chimp, that's what. Are you happy now?"

"Well . . ."

"Yeah, yeah. You don't have to say it, Morgan. It's written all over your face. All right, you and your pal here can go now. There's nothing more to talk about. Just one thing, Morgan . . ."

"Yes, Mr. Hackett?"

"No more monkeyshines, you hear me? I've got my eye on you. And I don't want no more funny business."

Morgan didn't say another word as he took Clarence by the hand and led him out of the office. If he were of a more demonstrative nature, he might have kicked up his heels and shouted "Yahoo!" as soon as he was out of earshot of Hackett. But that was not Morgan's way. Instead, he just tightened his grip on Clarence's hand and breathed a tremendous sigh of relief.

"That was a close one," he said. "But you're still here, Clarence, that's the important thing. And now I've got to figure out a way to *keep* you here." Clarence pursed his lips and chittered in agreement.

Daisy was the first to see them coming. "It's Clarence!" she cried to the others. "He's back!" An excited buzz traveled round the animals' cages. After all that William had told them, they never expected to see their friend again.

"Does this mean he's staying?" Ginger asked her mother.

"Well, I'm not sure, dear," replied Lucy. "It would certainly be salutary if it did, wouldn't it?"

"I don't know," said Ginger. "I don't know what that means."

Daisy regarded her friend Lucy with a mixture of amusement and exasperation. "She means," she said, turning to Ginger, "that it would be helpful to us if Clarence were to stay."

"Absolutely," agreed Lucy. "After all, we have yet to learn if Clarence has thought of a clever way out of our troubles. And, let's face it, we *need* him."

"Hear! Hear!" barked Basil. And the others nodded their accord.

By this time, Morgan had returned Clarence to his cage. Just as he was closing the door, Allison and Andrew came running toward him.

"Morgan! Morgan!" cried Andrew, trying to catch his breath. "We've been looking for you everywhere!"

"Yes," said Allison a little sternly. "Where have you been?"

"Oh, I've been having quite a day," replied Morgan, scratching his head. He told them then about everything that had happened—from his talk with the Mayor through Clarence's discovery and unexpected reprieve. "So you see," he said in conclusion, "it's been a day of mixed blessings."

"Yes," agreed Andrew. "But the important thing is that we still have two weeks."

"And that's why we've been looking for you," Allison said excitedly. "We have a plan."

Morgan raised an eyebrow. "A plan?" he asked.

"To save the zoo," said Andrew.

"Oh, dear," Morgan said, frowning. "I hope it's not like the last one. I'll never get away with anything like that again, what with Mr. Hackett watching over my shoulder and all."

"No, no," said Andrew, "it's nothing like that. It's a *terrific* plan. Our mom's going to do a story about the zoo closing."

"On television?" asked Morgan.

"Sure, on her news show," Andrew replied. "Isn't that great?"

"Well, yes. But how will her doing a story on the news save the zoo?"

"Don't you see, Morgan?" said Allison.

"She'll make it a real sad story, and then she'll tell everybody watching, 'If you don't want the zoo to close, call the Mayor! Send telegrams! Do something about it!' And then the zoo will be saved."

"Well, it *does* sound like a good plan," Morgan admitted. "And it's really nice of your mother to do it—"

Allison and Andrew looked at each other out of the corners of their eyes.

"What's wrong?" asked Morgan.

"Well," said Andrew slowly, "there's just one little problem."

"Oh?"

"Yes," said Allison. "See, our mother hasn't exactly . . . said . . . she would—"

"Oh."

"But she *will*," cried Andrew. "All we have to do is ask her. And we're going to do that tonight, aren't we, Allison?"

"Uh-huh. And she'll do it; she's just *got* to. And then everything will be all right, Morgan, you'll see."

The twins' eyes pleaded with Morgan to believe in their plan as strongly as they did. He wanted to, he really did, and as he looked into their earnest, upturned faces, he began to think it just might work.

"Tonight, you say?" he asked. "You're going to ask your mother tonight?"

"Yes," said Andrew.

"Tonight at supper," said Allison.

"And you think she'll agree to do it?"

"I *know* she will," Andrew said firmly. "She owes us one."

"What do you mean?" Morgan asked.

"Well, last week she ate the last two pieces of chocolate cake; they were supposed to be for us," replied Allison.

"Yeah," Andrew said, "so she owes us *something*, right?"

Morgan couldn't help but admire the twins' logic, if not their cunning. "All right," he said. "I'll see you tomorrow morning, then, and you'll let me know what happened."

The animals could hardly wait for Morgan and the twins to go home that night, so eager were they to discuss the possibilities that Allison's and Andrew's plan opened up. When at last they were alone, Lucy was the first to speak.

"Television!" she exclaimed. "We're going to be famous!"

"Well, I wouldn't go that far," commented Daisy.

"I was on television once," said Lucy, lapsing into the misty voice she used when recalling the days of her glorious (as she saw it) past. "It was the time the circus was celebrating its one hundredth year. I led a parade down Main Street, and then when we reached the coliseum where we were to play, I performed a little dance. It went something like this . . ." She lifted her front legs off the ground and, not without considerable effort, began a slow twirl in place.

If elephants could blush, Ginger would have turned crimson at that very moment. "Oh, Mother!" she said. "*Must* you?"

"It's all right, dear," said Daisy reassuringly. "Your mother is just excited. We *all* are. Not only will lots of people see us on this television show, but it could mean . . . yes, yes, it just could mean . . . that the zoo—"

"—will be saved!" said Gwen, overlapping Daisy's last words.

"Right!" Basil said. "But is it *enough* that people will see us? I mean to say, we're not that much to look at anymore. Just a bunch of middle-aged . . . with the exception of Ginger, of course . . .

mammals who have seen better days. And look at this place: it's as shabby as we are."

"Crabby?" grumbled Lance. "I can't help it if I'm crabby. You would be too if you had the kind of arthritis I've got."

"Basil didn't say 'crabby', dear," Gwen said gently. "He said we're 'shabby.' "

"Oh, *shabby*," said Lance, nodding. "Well, we're that, all right. But what do you expect? We're no spring chickens!"

Clarence had been silent through all of this, not because the conversation didn't interest him, but because he had been intently watching Lucy's cautious but graceful dance in the cage next door. It had given him an idea, one that he was now ready to share with the others.

"Excuse me, everyone," he said, clearing his throat.

All eyes were upon him at once.

"I agree with Basil that it isn't enough for people just to see this place, such as it is," he said. "What are we, after all? Just a bunch of ordinary animals in a zoo. But watching Lucy here has given me an idea."

Lucy dropped down to all four feet. "It has?" she cried. "Oh, how fortuitous!"

"I knew Clarence would come up with something," said Basil. "All right, old chap, let's hear it!"

"What if we were to show the world—or at least that part of it watching the news that night —that we are *not* such ordinary animals as we might seem? That we are in fact quite special?"

"How would we do that?" asked Daisy.

"Yes, old boy," Basil put in. "I mean to say, *we* know we're special, but how do we let everyone else know it?"

"By performing!" Clarence proclaimed.

"Performing!" echoed Lucy ecstatically. "Why, it'll be like the old days . . . it will be—"

"Yes, but what would we do?" asked Gwen. "Lucy has her little dance, but what could the rest of us do?"

"We'll each have to think of something," Clarence replied. "Something that will make people want to come and see us."

"But . . ." Gwen started to say.

"Let's sleep on it," Clarence suggested. "And tomorrow we'll talk about it some more. Don't worry, Gwen, we'll help each other out."

"We'll have to," replied Gwen. "Because I don't think there's anything Lance and I will be able to do. Oh, my, we lost that old get-up-and-growl a *long* time ago. And I'm afraid it's too late to get it back."

"Don't talk that way," said Daisy.

"No, no, it's true," Gwen said. "I'm just being realistic. We're the oldest ones here. And you know what they say: 'You can't teach an old cat new tricks.' "

No one had noticed that William was missing for most of this conversation. But he flew in just in time to hear what Gwen was saying. And it worried him. It worried him because of something Rollo Hackett had said a short time earlier to Morgan. Late that night, when everyone else was asleep, William told Clarence what he had overheard.

"Rollo Hackett has found homes for everyone here," he said. "Everyone, that is, but Lance and Gwen. They're so old nobody wants them."

"What will happen to them?" Clarence asked.

William looked across the way to be sure Lance and Gwen were sleeping and would not hear what he was about to say. "Mr. Hackett said that if he can't find a place for them," he murmured quietly, "they're to be put to sleep."

"What?" cried Clarence.

"Sshh."

"Put to sleep?" Clarence whispered. "You mean—?"

"Exactly," replied William.

Clarence looked over at Lance's and Gwen's cage. The two lions, snoring softly, were snuggled together and lost to the innocence of their slumber.

"We've got to help them," said Clarence resolutely. "We may not be able to save the zoo, but we've got to save Lance and Gwen."

William cooed in response. And like a ghost train the sound of it rode the still night air and sent a shiver of fear through the old lions' dreams.

6

The Old Days

THE NEXT MORNING arrived like an unexpected telegram. No one knew whether it held
good news or bad, but its very appearance
prompted a flurry of excitement and anticipation.

"I've had the most *oracular* dream!" Lucy exclaimed upon waking. "Ginger and I were dancing. We were wearing these adorable little
mother-and-daughter tutus, and we were bathed
in a glow of pink light. As we twirled round and
round, the crowd cheered and cheered! Suddenly, a man in a felt hat rushed through the
crowd and thrust a paper at us. 'Sign this con-

tract!' he shouted. 'I'm a talent scout and I'm going to make you the biggest stars since Weber & Fields!' "

"Who's that?" asked Gwen.

"I don't know, dear," Daisy replied. "She lost me back at the mother-and-daughter tutus."

"I had a dream, too," said Basil, clearing the early-morning cobwebs from his voice. "All of us seals," he went on, with a backward nod to the others in his pool, "were bouncing a brightly colored ball among us. A lot of people were watching us, laughing and clapping their hands. We were having such a good time, it reminded me of—"

"The old days!" cried Lucy. "Yes, yes, that's what my dream was like, too! The old days! Oh, wouldn't it be wonderful if—"

Suddenly Daisy gasped. "I just remembered what I had been thinking as I was drifting off to sleep last night," she said. "Do you remember . . . oh, I'm sure *all* of you must remember . . . when I was new here, and Morgan and I—"

"—played the bars of your cage!" said Gwen. "I remember! Oh, that was so much fun!"

"*I* don't remember," said Ginger. "What are you all talking about?"

"Why, this was before you were born, dear," Daisy said. "*Long* before you were born. What we're talking about is a little act Morgan and I used to do. I'd hold a stick between my teeth and tap the bars of my cage with it. With my long neck, I could move it about easily, you see. And while I was doing this, Morgan would hide behind a bush and play a little xylophone. Well, no one could see him, of course, so they thought that *I* was making the music. Oh, it's been so long since we did that. I wonder why we stopped."

"But you'll do it again, Daisy," said Clarence. "That's *just* the kind of thing we need. There, you see, I knew if we all slept on it, we'd come up with ideas."

"What about us?" Lance muttered. "We didn't have any fancy dreams like Lucy's there. And I don't think we'd be much good at bouncing a ball around on our noses."

"No," Clarence agreed. "Besides, I don't think that's what people would go for. They expect something else from lions." Recalling what William had told him the night before, Clarence regarded the ancient pair with a mixture of sadness and great determination. "You don't sup-

pose you could . . . roar," he suggested tentatively.

"Oh, good heavens!" sputtered Gwen. "We haven't had anything to roar about in so long, I'm sure we don't even remember how it's done."

"I could try," Lance said.

"Oh, my," said Gwen, a look of concern crossing her face. "Do you think you should? I mean, it might be dangerous . . . at your age."

"Nonsense!" Lance fairly exploded. If anything were going to encourage him, it was the intimation that he was too old. Scowling fiercely, he drew a vast amount of air in through his nostrils, expanded his chest and threw back his head. What emerged when he opened his mouth was not so much frightening in the way it called to mind the jungle as pitiful in the way it didn't. The sound of it fell somewhere between an asthmatic wheeze and a consumptive cough.

"Oh, dear," said Daisy softly. "Perhaps we'd better think of something else for Lance to do."

Basil agreed. "I'm afraid the only person that would impress," he said, "is a veterinarian!"

The outspoken seal had no sooner uttered those words than he regretted them. For now he watched as the old lion, his head hanging heavily, shuffled off to the far corner of his cage and sought refuge in its shadows. Gwen looked sorrowfully at the others, then took her place beside her mate, licking his mane as he licked his wounded pride.

William looked up at Clarence. "What are we going to do?" he whispered.

"I don't know," Clarence replied, shaking his head. "But we've got to think of *some*thing."

Suddenly an outburst of jubilant birdsong skittered through the air and tickled the eardrums of its listeners. William cocked his head. Had one of his exotic cousins escaped from the aviary? he wondered. Who could be making such a joyous sound?

Imagine everyone's surprise when Morgan appeared round the corner then, happily whistling, and swinging his buckets so effortlessly he might have been transporting bubbles rather than food.

"Good morning, everyone!" he called out. "Isn't it a glorious day?" The whistling continued as he went from cage to cage, distributing breakfast and good cheer. It was apparent that the twins' latest plan had filled Morgan with great hope.

"Shall we go for our constitutional?" he asked Clarence after the chimpanzee had finished eating. Clarence, chittering eagerly, swung through the tree branches that crisscrossed his cage until he came to the door. Morgan unlocked it quickly, and the two set off. When William looked up from the large piece of pizza crust with which he was wrestling, he observed that they were headed in the direction of the abandoned amusement area.

"JUNGLE PLAYLAND!" read the sign that arched over the entranceway to the amusement area. The words framed a large wooden elephant's head, its painted veneer worn away by rain and neglect. Facing Morgan and Clarence as they passed beneath it was an overgrown field filled with the tumbledown ghosts of rides and games that had once brought laughter to the lips of the children who had visited the zoo. Now, all was rusted metal and rotting wood and silence.

Morgan began to regret having come here this morning. He'd been feeling so good, so hopeful; now, he was surrounded by a blatant reminder that nothing lasts forever. And his hope began to fade. Looking back at the part of the zoo he had just left, he gripped Clarence's hand tightly.

"Just think," he said, "if Allison's and Andrew's plan doesn't work, the whole place will look like this soon. Mr. Hackett told me yesterday that he's found homes for all the animals, Clarence. Even you. Everybody but . . ." He let the sentence drift off as he sat down on an old storage trunk. The trunk had probably been used to hold prizes once: prizes for the most balloons broken, the closest bull's eye, the ring around the clown's nose. But it hadn't held anything in years, of course; the padlock hung open, rusty and useless.

Morgan sighed. "Remember that over there?" he asked Clarence, pointing to a circle of tiny buildings a few yards away. "That was the children's zoo, remember? We kept the baby animals there, and the boys and girls fed them from their own hands. Oh, they used to love that. Remember, Clarence? Baby deer and rabbits and pigs and . . . oh, this was quite a place once." He sighed again.

As Morgan continued to reminisce, Clarence ambled over to the children's zoo and jumped up onto the roof of one of the little houses. In times past when they had come here, Clarence had enjoyed leapfrogging from the top of one house to the next, going faster and faster until he had grown quite dizzy. He thought that might be a good bit of fun now and was just about to start when he noticed something glinting in the morning sun inside one of the buildings. He dropped down to the ground and poked his head inside. What he found was a tube of lipstick. He couldn't help but wonder where it had come from since the only people he knew who came here were Morgan and Rollo Hackett. But he didn't concern himself about it for long. Being a chimpanzee, he had a fondness for shiny objects. He decided to take it back with him and add it to the odds and ends he had collected from other walks.

Just then, he heard familiar cries.

"Morgan! Clarence!" Allison and Andrew were running toward them.

"Be careful," Morgan cautioned the twins. "There are all kinds of things hidden in this long grass. Don't trip now."

Clarence ran back to Morgan's side just as Allison and Andrew arrived.

"Oh, Morgan," said Allison, all out of breath,

"we have good news! Our mother said she'd do the story!"

"Really?" Morgan replied, his hope rising with his eyebrows.

"Yes," Andrew said. "We don't know when yet, 'cause she has to talk with her boss and get his okay. But she said that's just a . . . a tenna . . . a what, Allison?"

Allison's lips resisted the temptation to form a superior smile. "A technicality," she said.

"Right."

"Well, that's great news," said Morgan, smacking his hands together. "Great news. But we can't have the place looking the way it does now. Why, it's so rundown and . . . and . . . *pathetic,* no one's going to think it's worth saving." He stood then and looked off toward the animals' cages. "I've got to spruce it up, scrub it down, give it a little spit and polish!"

"We'll help!" cried Allison. "Won't we, Andrew?"

"You mean, like, work?"

"Sure, Andrew," said Morgan, "but it'll be fun. You'll see. We'll get this place looking like it hasn't for years."

"And we could fix it up like we were having

a party," suggested Allison, as the foursome began their brisk walk back. "You know, with balloons and streamers and—"

"Yeah," Andrew interjected, "and we could put up posters around town so that there'll be lots of people here."

" 'Come to the party at the zoo!' " shouted Allison.

"Come to the party at the zoo," Morgan echoed quietly. He shook his head in amazement at the thought. "We're going to do it!" he said, excitement overtaking him. "We're going to save the zoo. I just know we are. And it's going to be every bit as wonderful as the old days!"

"No way!" said Andrew.

Morgan looked at him in surprise.

Andrew smiled. "It'll be *better* than the old days!" he shouted.

Morgan, his eyes moist, began to laugh. And he laughed all the way back to Clarence's cage.

WILLIAM'S HEAD bobbed up and down and from side to side as he took in what Clarence was saying.

". . . and so," Clarence concluded, "they're

going to get lots of people to come here, and it'll be like a big party. It's perfect, don't you see, William? Now, tonight, after everyone goes home, we'll start practicing our acts so we'll be ready for the big day."

"But when *is* the big day?" William asked.

"We don't know yet, and that's where I need your help. Can you follow Allison and Andrew home tonight, William?"

"Sure."

"Their mother's going to tell them when she's coming here to do the story. If you can find that out, we'll know how much time we have."

All afternoon, Morgan and the twins scrubbed and lugged and patched and polished and painted. When it was time for Allison and Andrew to leave, they were tired but pleased with all that had been accomplished. The zoo was looking better already. They could hardly wait to return the next day and continue their work. But they were excited going home, too, for their mother was sure to have news for them—news of when their big party would take place. Excited and tired: it was a delicious jumble of feelings, one they savored the whole way home. And because they were so excited or because they were so tired, they never noticed that someone else was going home, too. A pigeon named William flew behind them all the way.

7

Tomorrow

WHEN ALLISON AND ANDREW Potter arrived home that night, an empty apartment awaited them. There was nothing unusual in this, of course, for their mother always worked late, what with her six o'clock news show and all. After letting themselves in, the twins ran immediately to the telephone answering machine to see if their mother had called and left any messages. Perhaps she had spoken with her boss and called to tell them what he'd said.

"Hi, kids," began the first (and only) message. "This'll have to be quick 'cause I'm running." ·

"This is it!" cried Allison hopefully.

"Sshh!" Andrew said. "Listen."

"I've made dentist appointments for both of you for Friday morning, so don't make any plans," the voice in the box went on. "And we should talk about getting you some clothes for school soon."

"Yeah, yeah," said Andrew impatiently. "But what about your boss? Did you talk to your boss?"

"Maybe this weekend we'll go shopping. Now, the reason I called . . ."

Allison and Andrew held their breaths.

". . . was to tell you that I'm going to be a little late tonight. I'll pick up some Chinese food on my way home. I'll see you about seven-fifteen. Hope you're having a good day. Call me if you need me. Love you." And a long, steady hum let the twins know their mother's message was over.

"Is that all?" asked Allison, disappointed.

"Boy, some message!" Andrew grumbled. "Dentist appointments and Chinese food. Great!"

"Do you think she forgot to talk to her boss?" Allison asked.

Andrew grabbed at a pillow from the sofa and pounded it with his fist. "I don't know," he said angrily. "All I know is we've had Chinese food an awful lot lately."

"Yes," agreed Allison. For a moment, she said nothing else. Then, quietly, she murmured, "Want to watch Mom's show? It's just about time."

"*You* watch," Andrew snapped. "I'm going to my room. Call me when the egg rolls get here."

From outside the window, William watched as Allison turned on the television and sat cross-legged before it, gazing at the two-dimensional image of the woman whose smiling face filled the screen. When, a short time later, that same woman emerged into the third dimension through the front door of the Potter apartment, Allison ran to greet her.

"I saw your show," she cried, as she did almost every night when her mother arrived home. "You looked so pretty."

"Oh, thank you, sweetheart," said Nan Potter, brushing a wayward strand of hair from her forehead. This she did with one hand; the other balanced an unwieldly bag mottled with spots of grease that grew and merged like multiplying amoebas. "I got your favorites," she said, handing the bag to her daughter.

Anxious as Allison was to know if her mother had spoken with her boss, she did not rush to ask her. She could see that Nan was tired; more than that, she understood that something was wrong. It was nothing her mother had said in the few minutes she'd been home; it was in the way her hands kept pushing the hair out of her eyes, the way her lips were pulled tight, the way her eyes looked at Allison and didn't see her.

"I'll put this on the table," Allison said.

"Let's eat out on the terrace," said her mother. "It's such a beautiful night."

Now, it was lucky for William that Allison's mother made this suggestion, for up until now he had been unable to hear a single word that had been spoken. When he saw the twins and Nan Potter coming toward the door to the terrace, he quickly ducked into a carton that was tipped on its side and listened attentively.

"I'm sorry you're sick of Chinese food, Andrew," Nan was saying as she opened the door.

"To tell you the truth, I'm getting a little tired of it myself. But, with everything that's been going on at the station, it's all I can manage these days." Andrew, shoulders hunched and hands shoved resolutely into the pockets of his dungarees, grunted.

Silently, Allison helped her mother open the white containers of wonton soup and egg rolls and moo shu pork. They dished out portions for everyone, but as the two children began to eat, Nan only jabbed at the egg roll lying on her plate. Like a fish refusing to be harpooned, it artfully dodged each stab of the chopstick.

"Don't play with your food, Mom," Andrew couldn't resist saying. Nan smiled weakly and lifted the egg roll to her mouth. But she didn't take a bite.

"It just kills me," she said then. "They complain about the ratings, but they don't let me do anything about it."

"What?" said Allison softly.

"Oh, it's our ratings again, honey," her mother replied. "The station is falling behind, and the news show is the lowest it's been in a long, long time."

"*I* like it, Mom."

"Thanks, Allison. I wish more people did."

"I do, too," Andrew said.

"Well, that's two," said Nan with half a smile. "Now, we just need a few thousand more. I keep telling them nobody cares about the kind of news we do, but they don't listen. And then they yell at *me* when the ratings drop."

"News is news, isn't it, Mom?" asked Allison.

"Well, yes, in a way. But it's also a matter of *which* news you show. Take today, for instance. Today, there was a big robbery at the Rutherford House." Allison and Andrew recognized the name as the home of one of the city's wealthiest families. "A fortune in jewelry was stolen, and no one knows how. They think it was two people— a man and a woman—but they're not even sure of that. Anyway, the point is, we didn't get the story. Every other station had it as their lead item on the six o'clock news. What was our lead? The gala opening of a new beauty parlor for poodles! *That*'s the kind of news they want me to cover, and then they wonder why our ratings are so low."

This last statement was punctuated by a loud crunch as Nan took an angry bite of her egg roll. Allison and Andrew glanced nervously at each other across the table. The way their mother was talking, there was little hope she would want to do a story on the zoo.

"Oh, by the way," Nan said then, as if reading her children's thoughts, "I talked to Mr. Bailey today about covering the closing of the zoo and—"

"And he said 'forget it,' right?" Andrew remarked a little abruptly.

"Oh, on the contrary," his mother replied. "He loved the idea. After all, that's his favorite kind of story." The two children broke into relieved smiles. "There's only one catch . . ." Their smiles froze. "He wants me to wait until next week."

"But why?" asked Andrew.

"That leaves less than a week until the zoo is supposed to close," Allison said plaintively.

"I know, I know," said Nan, "but he has other stories he wants me to do first. Besides, I'm really trying to convince him that our show needs a little more punch, a little more pizazz."

"This story's got punch!" exclaimed Andrew. "It's got what-d'ya-callit!"

"What I'm trying to say, Andrew, is that we need stories that are more *important*."

"But, Mom!" cried Andrew, jumping up from his chair. "This story *is* important. Don't you see?"

"I'm sure it is to you," Nan replied wearily, "but—"

Allison began to clear the dishes. "What matters," she said quietly, "is that Mom is going to do the story, even if it isn't right away. Anyway, Andrew, this just gives us more time to help Morgan get the zoo ready. After all, we want to put up posters and make the place look nice, don't we?"

"Well, yeah . . ."

"So it's even better this way. Now, when the zoo is shown on TV, it'll look great, and there'll be lots of people there. Right?"

"You're right," said Andrew, convinced by his sister's logic. Turning to Nan, he said, "Thanks, Mom."

"Yeah, Mom," Allison said, "thanks."

Nan put out her arms and drew her children to her. "I haven't been such a great mother lately, have I?" she asked without waiting for a reply. "I'm sorry, kids. As soon as I get out from under, I'll make it up to you, I really will." She smiled then and gave the twins a squeeze. "And, meanwhile," she said, "we'll do the best darn story on that zoo you can imagine. We'll make 'em laugh, we'll make 'em cry. But most important, we'll make 'em care. They won't let the zoo close when I'm through with them, kids—that's a promise!"

THE NEXT FEW DAYS seemed to whiz by. Once the animals learned from William when the television people would be coming, they threw themselves into the pleasurable task of rehearsing their acts. Lucy, nearly dizzy from happiness at the thought that her "comeback" was only days away, busied herself teaching Ginger half-remembered dance steps from her youth. What she couldn't recall she improvised. Ginger, feeling awkward in the way adolescents do, was reluctant to follow her mother's lead at first. She didn't want to appear foolish, she said. But once she was convinced that her participation in the big event was vital, she overcame her resistance and discovered, much to her amazement, that she actually enjoyed dancing. "Show business is in your blood," her mother told her dramatically.

The seals did not have as easy a time getting their act underway, for Morgan didn't understand what they were trying to tell him at first.

When he noticed them tossing their fish about at feeding time, he thought perhaps they were fighting over their food. But after a day or two, he gathered from their playful barks that they were amusing themselves. "What they need is a toy," he decided. And then it was no time at all before they were bouncing a brightly colored ball (much like the one in Basil's dream) from nose to nose and creating intricate patterns of play that were bound to delight the crowd that would surround their pool on the big day.

It took even more doing, however, to resurrect Daisy's xylophone act. Morgan seemed to be at a total loss to comprehend what it was she was trying to communicate each time he came to feed her. Perhaps she was not making herself clear enough as she tapped the bars of her cage with a stick; more likely, Morgan had forgotten altogether the game they used to play. Then Clarence decided that Morgan could not be depended upon to perform with Daisy even if he did catch on.

"After all," Clarence reasoned, "when the big day gets here, Morgan's mind is bound to be on other things. So *I'll* do the act with you, Daisy."

"But you'll need a xylophone," Daisy replied sensibly.

And so whenever Morgan passed by his cage, the chimpanzee played an imaginary xylophone, hoping Morgan would get the hint and provide him with a real one. Morgan didn't. It was not until Andrew and Allison happened to spot Clarence's pantomine one day that he met with success.

"Look!" cried Allison. "Clarence looks just like you, Andrew."

"Thanks a lot," Andrew said.

"No, no, I mean the way you looked when you were little . . . when you played your toy xylophone."

"Yeah, you're right," agreed Andrew. "Maybe he'd like one. I'll give him mine. I don't need it anymore."

And so it was that Clarence became the proud owner of a slightly used but musically sound xylophone. He and Daisy began practicing their act at once. And soon, their little corner of the zoo rocked with laughter as the other animals watched Clarence hang upside down from a branch and boisterously pound out a melody while Daisy, a twig clamped like a cigar between her teeth, swung her long neck back and forth and "played" the tune on the bars of her cage.

The only ones *not* preparing for the big day were Lancelot and Guenevere. Ever since Lance's pitiful exhibition, no one had dared to suggest again that they roar. Yet no one, not even Clarence, had come up with any other way for them to prove how special they were. From time to time, Gwen confided her concern to her friend, Daisy.

"It's not myself I'm worried about," she said one morning. "It's Lance. Once, when his mane was full and shining with life, when his limbs were strong and his growl rich and deep, he was the pride of the zoo. Do you remember, Daisy? People used to crowd round our cage, and if Lance so much as lifted his head, they'd pull back in fear and respect. Now, he just sleeps all day and barely lifts his head at all. Oh, what are we going to do?"

Daisy regarded the venerable old lioness fondly. Suddenly, an idea occurred to her. "Maybe you don't have to do anything but be yourselves," she suggested.

"What do you mean?" asked Gwen.

"Why, I see how the two of you are—always snuggling up together and licking each other. I'll bet people would be touched watching two old lions who so obviously care for each other."

"Well," said Gwen, considering the idea, "I don't see what we have to lose. After all, it *is* the one thing we do well. And just think, we won't even have to practice!" Feeling relieved, Gwen returned to her mate's side.

For Morgan and the twins, meanwhile, there was much to be done in what seemed an impossibly short period of time. What was broken was mended, what was dirty was cleaned, what was worn with age was rejuvenated with plaster and paint. With his own money, Morgan rented a pump and bought balloons, and with some of their savings, Allison and Andrew bought posterboard and colored pens. The day before Nan and her television crew were to arrive, the twins put up posters all over the neighborhood.

"Come To The Party At The Zoo!" shouted the red felt-tip letters. "Free Balloons!" cried the yellow. "Elephants! Lions! Monkeys!" screamed the green. "Tomorrow Is the Day!" sang the multi-colored chorus.

The zoo itself was now festooned with streamers that fluttered in the wind and resembled, in Morgan's assessment, a madcap carousel spinning dizzily in a dream. After the last streamer had been hung, the last drop of paint dried, the last brass railing polished, the three exhausted workers stepped back to admire all that they had done. They were exhilarated by the anticipation of tomorrow. *Tomorrow:* almost here at last. Nothing, not even Rollo Hackett grumbling about their wasting time and energy or mumbling about the "stupidity" of bringing television cameras to the zoo, could dampen their spirits.

"See you tomorrow," the twins said to Morgan, when at last it was time for them to go.

"Yes," he replied, returning their smile. "Tomorrow."

"Tomorrow," said Clarence to the other animals that evening, "is our big day. Let's all get a good night's sleep and greet the morning with hope—hope that tomorrow we will be saved."

"Tomorrow a star will be born," Lucy told her daughter as they drifted off to sleep. And perhaps, she told herself, another star will be born again.

"Tomorrow we'll play ball like we've never played before," Basil began his pep talk to the other seals. "And we'll make the crowd laugh and laugh and . . ."

"Tomorrow the crowd will laugh and applaud," Daisy was saying to Gwen as they bid each other goodnight. "Oh, how they used to laugh. And, tomorrow, they will again. As for you . . ."

Gwen looked up anxiously at her friend. "Yes?" she asked.

"Tomorrow people will come to see two lions, and they'll stay to learn about love."

Gwen regarded her sleeping mate affectionately. "Goodnight," she whispered to Daisy. "Until tomorrow."

LATE THAT NIGHT, Morgan sat up in bed staring into the shadows that draped the corners of his room. Across from him, atop a simple oak dresser (his mother's once; he recalled watching her standing before it combing out her long auburn hair), were photographs in dime-store frames. Most were of himself with the animals at the zoo. His favorite was of Clarence, perched on Morgan's shoulders piggy-back fashion and peeking out from under the zookeeper's cap, which was cocked over one eye. His gaze drifted now to the leather-bound rocker, its seat torn and stitched and torn again. He thought of his father sitting there, holding him on his lap, excitedly describing his new job on the railroad . . . the job that took him so far away so many times. Morgan imagined he heard the chug-chug-chug of a train, but it was only the tick-tick-tick of his clock.

Three a.m. He couldn't sleep. Memories of his parents floated through his mind like ghosts come to remind him that old men were children once. And children grew and left their parents behind and had children of their own. He got up, crossed the room, picked up the picture of Clarence. He smiled, looking at it; then frowned, telling himself it was foolish to think of a chimpanzee as his child. But who else was there to fill Morgan's days? Who else to fill the dime-store frames atop his bureau? Who but the animals? The animals . . .

So much depends on tomorrow, Morgan thought, as he got back into bed. He turned out the light and was plunged into a sea of black. Tomorrow, he thought as he surfaced to the light of the moon through the window. Tomorrow. And the word echoed softly until it became a dream and he was asleep.

8

"Save Our Zoo!"

EIGHT O'CLOCK. The morning sky, a field of perfect blue, was marred only by a single gray cloud that had strayed into a flock of white. Something else gray and alone floated in the air above the zoo, and that was a pigeon . . . a pigeon so anxious to see the day begin that he had taken flight in hopes of getting a better view.

From where he hovered, William watched the zoo come to life. Animals stretched and yawned, rolled heavily from side to side, raised themselves at last on wobbly legs and shook the straw and sleep from their bodies. And then, as if suddenly remembering that this was a *special* day, they began to pace their cages and look out eagerly for the arrival . . . the arrival of what? Perhaps, as with William, the arrival of the day itself. Even Lance and Gwen, so rarely roused to action, moved restlessly from one end of their cage to the other. Their tails snapped at the air, stinging it with impatience; their bowed heads brushed against each other as if to soothe away their nervousness.

All the animals were nervous, of course. William could see in their agitation that they only wanted the crowds to assemble, the television cameras to roll, the moment to arrive when they would perform their acts and, by performing, capture the city's imagination and thereby save themselves. But that was all hours away. The television people would not be coming until early in the afternoon and it was now only early in the morning.

From the corner of his eye, William noticed a sudden movement. He looked down and saw, much to his surprise, that the ordinarily deserted Jungle Playland was *not* deserted this morning. Three figures—men, it appeared—were walking toward the children's zoo. One man, wearing a red hat (it was this that had caught William's attention), was pounding the fist of one hand into the palm of the other. William could not hear the man's words but he concluded from his gestures that he was speaking angrily. One of the other men kept shaking his head, as if to deny whatever it was the man in the red had was telling him. The third man, his long arms dangling at his sides, kicked at the dirt as he walked and seemed to have nothing to say.

No one ever comes to this part of the zoo, William thought. What were these three men doing here, especially at this hour? He was all set to fly down and investigate when he heard a commotion elsewhere. The animals were heralding Morgan's arrival. William, anxious to join his friends, decided that he would investigate another time. Or perhaps he needn't bother. After all, he told himself as he flew away, the men he had seen were possibly just three homeless souls who had spent the night in the park. If that were the case, they were more cause for compassion than concern. And so he thought no more about it.

TEN-THIRTY. Allison and Andrew, breathless with excitement, arrived carrying a large roll of white fabric between them.

"Look!" they cried to Morgan, who was re-hanging some streamers that had come undone in the previous night's wind. "We made a sign!" They unfurled their banner, formerly a bed-sheet, and held it up for Morgan's appraisal.

"SAVE OUR ZOO!" read the hand-painted sign the twins had spent much of the past week making.

"Impressive," Morgan said. "Very impressive."

Turning to each other, the animals nodded their approval.

"Where can we hang it?" Andrew asked. "Our mom said she'd be sure the camera gets a good shot of it. So we have to put it someplace it'll be seen."

Morgan stroked his chin as he surveyed the area. "How about over there?" he suggested, pointing to an area next to the seal pool. "We can suspend it from this tree to that lamppost."

Basil and his ball-bouncing companions exchanged satisfied glances. Now, they'd be *certain* to be noticed.

ONE O'CLOCK. Morgan shook his head in amazement as he beheld a sight he had not witnessed

for many years. The zoo was teeming with people. The posters had worked! Bewildered infants, strapped like papooses onto their fathers' backs, peeked out from behind bushy heads of hair to gaze and wonder. Toddlers who had never before seen anything quite like an elephant squealed with delight as Lucy and Ginger went into their dance. Children a little younger than Andrew and Allison raced about holding tight the free balloons the twins had handed them when they'd entered the zoo. Young couples, arms interwined, interrupted their surveys of each other's features long enough to look and laugh when Daisy, with Clarence's help, "played" the bars of her cage. And older couples, having memorized their partner's features long ago, were content to stand and stare at Lance and Gwen, no doubt seeing in the gentle, loving creatures reflections of themselves.

And the air was filled with words Morgan wished he could grab and collect and stuff into an envelope to send off to the Mayor.

"What a great place this is!"

"I haven't had this much fun in a long time."

"We have to come again."

"I *like* it here, Mommy."

Suddenly, Morgan was inspired. Why hadn't he thought of it before? He ran to the office, grabbed a clipboard, a pencil and some paper, and hastily wrote at the top:

Dear Mayor Thayer,
 We the undersigned citizens of this great city protest the closing of the Chelsea Park Zoo. What a great place this is! We haven't had so much fun in a long time. We *like* it here, Mr. Mayor. Please keep the zoo open!

Satisfied with what he had written, he rushed out the door and crashed into Rollo Hackett.

"Watch where you're going," Hackett snapped.

Morgan hastily picked up the fallen clipboard and dusted it off. "Excuse me, Mr. Hackett," he said. "I was in a hurry. I didn't see you. I—"

"Yeah, well . . ." Rollo Hackett said indifferently. A great crease furrowed his brow. He seemed worried, preoccupied. He tugged at his hat and mumbled something Morgan didn't understand.

"I have to be going," Morgan said, eager to return to the crowd with his petition.

"Yeah, I'm sure you do," said Hackett. "You're having a high old time, aren't you, Morgan? Kidding yourself that this grandstand play of yours is going to make any difference. I don't like it, Morgan. I don't like all these people here, and I don't like television butting its nose in. It's an invasion of privacy, that's what it is."

"What are you talking about, Mr. Hackett?" Morgan could not help but reply. "This is a public place and the closing of the zoo is a matter of public concern. Or at least we're trying to make it into one."

"Well, try all you like, Morgan. It won't get you anywhere. Just leave me out of it, you understand? I don't want any part of this publicity stunt of yours. I *hate* publicity, Morgan. Especially when it's for something nobody gives a hoot about."

Morgan did not intend to argue the point any further with Rollo Hackett, who seemed to be in an even grumpier mood than usual. He ran off toward the crowd, waving his clipboard in the air.

"Sign our petition!" he cried. "Save the zoo!"

TWO O'CLOCK. Morgan had collected eighty-seven names. Allison and Andrew had given away all the balloons there were to give. The crowd was beginning to thin out and go home. And there was no sign of Nan Potter or her television crew.

"What time did you say they were supposed to be here?" Morgan asked the twins.

"Mom said they'd be here by one o'clock," replied Allison. "I don't understand it. She's usually on time for things. Or she lets us know she's going to be late."

"I wish she'd hurry up," Andrew said, scowling.

"So do I," Allison agreed.

Morgan had to admit he was growing a little anxious, too. He glanced up at the sky. The single gray cloud had been joined by a host of others. It seemed as if it might pour any minute.

THREE O'CLOCK. Allison, a glum expression on her face, put down the telephone receiver.

"They said she's out on an assignment," she

reported, turning to her brother and Morgan. "But they wouldn't say where. They said they didn't think she was at the zoo—"

"Thanks a lot, guys," snapped Andrew. "I think we had that one figured out."

"They said something came up, but they wouldn't say what."

Morgan and the twins left the office and returned to the nearly empty compound. A light drizzle was beginning to come down.

"I'm sure they'll be here yet," Morgan said, more to himself than anyone else. "It'll be all right. Even if there aren't a lot of people here, even if it's raining a little, even —"

A crash of thunder cut off the rest of Morgan's sentence. And the heavens opened up. While the few remaining visitors ran for cover, Morgan and the twins stood where they were and watched their streamers tear and collapse under the weight of the rain. They saw the animals cower from the sudden storm and retreat to the backs of their cages. They observed the colors drain from the words "SAVE OUR ZOO!" and run off the edges of the drenched banner to form rainbow rivers on the pavement below.

SIX O'CLOCK. Morgan turned on the old black-and-white television set that sat atop the filing cabinet in Rollo Hackett's office. Hackett had disappeared from sight earlier that afternoon. The storm raging outside made the usually poor reception even poorer. But, though the static twitched and buzzed like a swarm of angry mosquitoes, the zookeeper and the twins were able to make out the face of Nan Potter.

" 'When news happens, we happen to be there'," she was saying.

"Oh, yeah?" Andrew mumbled. "You didn't happen to be *here* today."

"Today's big story: Jewelry thieves strike again! Today's victim was society biggie, Leticia Brickle. Widow of famed bandleader, 'Bucky' Brickle, the feisty (and fabulously wealthy) octogenarian was returning from an archery lesson when she noticed two people shimmying down the rainpipe outside her rear pantry. 'If I'd had my bow and arrow with me,' she is quoted as saying, 'I would have nailed them myself.' Ms. Brickle and her chauffeur, Rodney, have told police that the thieves were a man of medium stature and a tall dark-haired woman. Police estimate that the thieves made off with over a million dollars in gems."

Andrew walked to the television set and, with a flick of his fingers, banished his mother from the room. "Well, I hope Mom's happy," he said. "She finally got her big story."

For a long time, no one said another word. They just listened to the sound of the falling rain and thought their own thoughts.

EIGHT O'CLOCK. Morgan and the twins had gone home. The animals, huddled in their cages, looked out at the rain, which gave no sign of stopping.

"Well," Lucy said to Clarence through the bars of their adjoining cages, "today certainly proved one thing."

"What's that?" Clarence asked.

"You can't trust anyone," the elephant replied with a sigh. "Especially *people*."

Clarence was not sure he agreed. But one thing he felt as deeply in his bones as the chill that the rain had brought with it: unless something unexpected happened, there was little hope left of saving the zoo.

9

Something Unexpected

As if by unspoken agreement, Morgan and the animals woke the next morning determined to make the most of the time left to them. After all, there was nothing more they could do; their hopes had been washed away in yesterday's rain. When the zookeeper arrived at the animals' cages, he was swinging his buckets and whistling a tune as if this day, one of the few remaining to the Chelsea Park Zoo, were no different from any other. A half-hour later, he and Clarence set off on their constitutional.

"What have we here?" Morgan asked, as they

passed by the Jungle Playland entrance. Inside
the gate, sitting astride a weather-beaten seesaw,
were two men playing cards. Morgan and Clarence, hand in hand, entered the amusement area
and approached them.

"Good morning," said Morgan.

The two men looked up, startled.

"G'morning," said the beefier of the two. His
companion, a tall, stringy fellow, said nothing.
Yet his eyes darted nervously about as he
kneaded the flesh of his smooth, hairless chin
between thumb and forefinger.

"Just out for our constitutional," Morgan
went on. "Clarence and I always go for a walk
after breakfast."

"Uh-huh," grunted the stocky one. "You . . .
uh . . . you work for the zoo, huh?"

"Oh, yes," Morgan replied amiably. "I have
for many years. *Many* years. But it looks like I'll
be out of a job soon. The zoo's going to close, you
know. At least, that's what they say."

"Yeah," said the man, scratching himself
with such vigor Clarence couldn't help wondering if he had fleas. "We know the zoo's closin'.
That's why we're here. We're waitin' for Mr.
Hackett."

"Oh?" said Morgan.

"Yeah, we're supposed t'start taking this place apart. Dis*mant*le it, y'understand?"

"Oh, dear," Morgan said. "I do understand. I hadn't realized . . . that is, it never occurred to me . . . that the zoo was actually going to be torn down." He sighed heavily and looked for empathy from Clarence, but the chimpanzee was momentarily preoccupied by something he'd spotted in the grass a few feet away.

"Is this your first day of work?" Morgan asked the two men. The silent one continued to pull at his chin as if to force a beard out of hiding. The other man picked at his teeth with an ace of diamonds.

"Yeah," he said. "First day."

Clarence let go of Morgan's grip and wandered off to pick up the shiny object from where it lay. He turned it over in his hand, unsure what to make of it, and returned to the zookeeper.

"Well," said Morgan, "I expect you'll be starting your labors here in the amusement area."

"That's right. Right here. Don't worry, pal, we won't be botherin' you none. We won't even get to the other part o' the zoo till you and the beasts is gone."

Morgan turned suddenly at the sound of footsteps behind him. It was Rollo Hackett.

"What are you doing here?" Hackett asked Morgan. "And what's that ape doing out of his cage? Oh, never mind. I don't even want to know. Well, men," he went on, turning his attention to the two cardplayers, "you ready to work?"

"Yes, sir, Mr. Hackett," replied the stocky one. His abrupt rise from the seesaw sent his partner crashing to the ground. The cards flew into the air and landed, helter-skelter, on and around the befuddled man. Rollo Hackett and the other man broke out laughing with such force that they were soon holding their stomachs and wiping the tears from their eyes. The man on the ground found nothing to laugh at. Trying to regain his dignity, he stood and brushed himself off. As he did so, Clarence noticed something fall from his pocket.

"Come on," Rollo Hackett said at last, pulling his hat down over his forehead, "we've got work to do. And so do you, Morgan."

"Yes, sir, Mr. Hackett."

As the three men walked away, Clarence ran to where he had seen the item fall from the tall man's pocket. Spotting it in the grass, he was surprised to discover that it was identical to the thing he had found a moment earlier.

"Come along, Clarence," Morgan said, calling his friend. "It's time for me to get back to work. Our walk will have to be a little shorter than usual today."

Clarence picked up the found object, put it with the other in his hand, and returned with Morgan to his cage.

"I don't know what they're called," William told Clarence a short time later, "but I think they're something girls wear in their hair."

Clarence looked down at the shiny objects in his hand. "What makes you say so?" he asked the pigeon.

"Well, I'm not positive," William replied. "But it seems to me I've seen Allison pull back her hair and fasten it with things a lot like these."

Clarence was puzzled. "That's strange," he said. "Why would that man be carrying girls' hair-things in his pocket?"

William ruffled his feathers, the pigeon

equivalent of a shrug. "Maybe he was holding them for his wife or daughter and forgot he had them," he said.

"Mmm," said Clarence, thinking it over, "you're probably right." Suddenly, he let out a great sigh.

"What's the matter?" William asked.

Clarence shook his head. "Oh, I don't know," he said. "I guess it's just hard to believe that the zoo is really coming to an end. They're tearing the place down, William. Did I tell you that?"

William nodded.

"They're starting today over in the amusement area. They won't tear this part of the zoo down till we're gone." He smiled ruefully. "At least we'll be spared watching our homes turned to rubble," he said. "That's something, I suppose."

William and Clarence fell silent. Together, the two friends gazed across the way at Daisy nibbling on some leaves, at Lance and Gwen stretching their aging muscles. For the first time, the pigeon wondered what he would do when the zoo closed down. Where would he go? Perhaps, he thought, he'd follow Clarence to his new home. After so many years, it was impossible to imagine life without him.

IN AN APARTMENT not far from the zoo, meanwhile, a mother and two children sat eating their breakfast. The only sounds to be heard were the steady crunching of cereal and the occasional slurping of milk or juice. The mother, who would ordinarily have admonished her children for making such noises when they drank, said nothing. And the children, who on most mornings were full of animated conversation, sat like bookends on either side of their mother and stared down at their bowls as if they might find there the answer to some unasked question.

The mother's spoon clinked the sides of her glass mug as she stirred her coffee. At last, she spoke.

"I don't blame you for being mad at me," she said. "What I did was a terrible thing. I told you I was coming yesterday, and then I didn't show up. I didn't even call. And that wasn't fair or thoughtful of me. But I hope you'll try to understand *why* I did what I did."

"You told us already," Andrew mumbled.

"Yes," said his twin, "you told us last night."

"I know I did," Nan Potter said, "but I don't feel you really understand. For the first time in months, I had the chance to get a *real* story—something important, something that might help the station's ratings. I had to go after it, don't you see? Even if I hadn't wanted to, my boss would have insisted."

Andrew shoved his empty cereal bowl forward on the table. "You keep talking about *important* stories, *real* stories," he said angrily. "And we keep telling you this story *is* real and important. But you don't care. If you did, you would have been there."

"I *do* care," Nan replied. "I guess I just don't understand why it's so important to you. I know you like the zoo, and I'm sorry it's closing, but it's not the *only* thing in your lives."

"Your job isn't the only thing in your life, either," Andrew snapped. "But it sure seems to matter an awful lot to you."

Nan was stung by the sharpness of her son's remark. She wanted to tell him to watch what he said, but she couldn't help but recognize the truth in his words.

"The zoo's important to us," Allison said

softly, "because Morgan and the animals are our friends. We really know them and we like them and we don't want them to move away."

"Besides," Andrew said, "it's not just us we're thinking about. The zoo is the animals' home. They've lived there all their lives. And Morgan has taken care of them since they were born. Just think how you'd feel if somebody came along and sent Allison and me to new homes far away from you and far away from each other so that none of us ever saw each other again. That'd be pretty lousy, wouldn't it, Mom?"

Nan sighed. "Yes," she agreed, "it would." She looked into her children's eyes. "I won't promise anything," she said, "because I don't want to break another promise. But I'll speak to Mr. Bailey again and see if I can still do the story. I don't know if he'll agree and I don't know when he'll let me do it, but I'll try."

Suddenly, a buzzer sounded.

"That's your father," said Nan Potter. "Hurry along now. You don't want to keep him waiting."

After the twins had left to join their father for a day of movies and museums and pizza and ice cream, Nan poured herself a second mug of coffee. She sat at the kitchen table for a long time that morning, just sipping her coffee and thinking.

WILLIAM SPENT a good part of his morning thinking, too. But, now, as Clarence and the others settled in for their early afternoon naps, he grew restless and decided to give his wings a little exercise. He set off in the direction of the amusement area, curious to know how work was progressing.

When he first spotted them, the three men were clumped together inside the children's zoo pitching cards into Rollo Hackett's red hat. He could see that Hackett and another man, a short, stocky character in a checkered jacket, were in the middle of a lively discussion. The third man, tall and lanky, stood off to the side. Something was draped over his left hand; William couldn't make it out exactly, but it looked like a large piece of brown cloth. The pigeon looked about and was struck by the fact that the amusement area didn't appear any different from when he'd seen it last. It was then that he realized he hadn't heard any sounds coming from the place all morning. Surely, the tearing apart of wood and concrete and metal would have made enough noise to travel to the animals' cages. And now that he thought about it, where were the workers' tools? From what Clarence had told him and what he now saw with his own eyes, playing cards were the tools of *their* trade. And where had he seen that red hat before?

"Listen," Rollo Hackett was saying as William came down for a landing, "it's the perfect set-up. Anybody can see that."

"That's what's got me worried," said the stocky man, tossing a card in the direction of the hat. "Anybody *can* see it. I didn't like that what's-his-name snoopin' around here this morning."

"Who, Morgan?" Hackett said. "Don't worry about him. He's a sap. He'll believe whatever I want him to believe."

"But shouldn't we be doing something? I mean, what's he gonna think with us just hangin' around and all? If we're supposed t'be tearin' the place apart—"

"You never heard of *planning*?" said Rollo Hackett. The card he tossed sailed through the air and landed neatly in the center of the hat. "Well, that's what we're doing. If anybody asks, and I doubt they're going to, we say we're in the planning stages of the . . . uh . . . what'd'ya callit . . . the demolition of the zoo. After all," he said, tapping his forehead, "you gotta think before you act. Right?"

The stocky man shrugged. "If you say so," he said. "You're the brains."

A snakelike smile slithered across Hackett's face. "And don't you forget it," he said.

The tall man tossed a card, then returned to running his fingers through the object in his hand. Close up, William saw that it wasn't cloth the man held, but hair. Hackett and the other man were watching him, too.

The man in the checkered coat shook his head. "Geez, Duffy," he said, "you and that wig. It's a good thing Morgan didn't see you with that thing. He woulda *known* somethin' weird was going on."

"Don't worry about Duffy," said Rollo Hackett. "He's all right."

"Sure, he's all right," grunted the other man. "Just plays with that wig all day and never says nothin'. And this morning, he was all in a huff 'cause he lost his barrettes."

"His what?" Hackett asked.

"His barrettes. You know, those things girls

put in their hair. I don't know, Duffy, maybe you shoulda been born a girl."

Barely was this last word spoken than Rollo Hackett grabbed the short man by the lapels. "I told you not to worry about Duffy," he growled. "Now lay off." He pushed the man away and brushed himself off as if he were the one who'd been attacked. "Now, c'mon," he said, "let's get some eats. I'm starved."

William watched as the three men picked up their cards and walked away. He heard the stocky man say to Rollo Hackett, "You're sure everything's gonna be all right? Everytime that trunk is outa my sight, I get nervous."

Hackett started to laugh. "I never knew anybody who worried as much as you," he said slapping the man on the back. "You'd make somebody a great mother. And you talk about Duffy." Duffy trailed behind, still combing his fingers through the dark wig. William couldn't hear the other man's response to Rollo Hackett because the sound of their voices was growing faint in the distance.

With a great flutter, the pigeon became airborne. His thoughts were a tangle of all that he'd just seen and heard, and he needed Clarence to help sort them out. One thing was certain: Rollo Hackett and the two "workmen" were up to something and, from the sound of it, it wasn't good.

10

Cheerio, Clarence!

"You're right," Clarence said to William when the pigeon had finished speaking. "Something *is* going on. And I have a pretty good idea what."

"You do?" William asked. He cooed with relief at the thought that some sense might be made of the confusion buzzing along his brainwaves.

Clarence nodded slowly. "Yes," he said. "It all fits with something I heard Morgan and the twins talking about. Especially that business of the trunk. You see . . . wait a minute, what's this all about?"

William looked up to see that Morgan and his boss had entered the compound. They stopped before Daisy's cage as Rollo Hackett flipped through the pages of the notebook he was holding in his hands. He mumbled something neither Clarence nor William could make out. The first words they heard, the next words spoken, were Morgan's.

"Next Wednesday?" he said. He looked up at Daisy and added, a little mournfully, "That's so soon."

"Yeah, well, you'd better get used to the idea, Morgan," Hackett said, not lifting his eyes from the page. "After all, the zoo's closing Tuesday. Now, where was I? Oh, yeah, one giraffe, female, to Kalamazoo. On Wednesday." He scribbled something in the notebook and moved away. Clarence and William watched as Hackett, followed closely by Morgan, approached the elephants' cage.

"Okay," Hackett said, turning a page in the notebook. "Let's see what the story is on these two. One elephant, female," he said, raising his eyebrows as he looked up, "getting along in years . . ."

Lucy exchanged a glance with Clarence. "Well, I never!" her eyes seemed to say.

" . . . going to San Diego. As for the, you should pardon the expression, *little* one, she's set for Rochester."

"New York?" asked Morgan, taken aback.

Hackett consulted his notes. "Yep," he said, "that's the place."

Looking into Ginger's eyes, Morgan was sure he saw tears forming there. "But . . . but," he stuttered, "they'll be across the country from each other."

Hackett just shook his head at the zoo-keeper's sentimentality. "What difference would it make if they were across the *street*?" he asked. "They're not gonna be visiting each other."

"But I didn't know they were going to be separated," said Morgan. "You didn't tell me that."

"I don't tell you everything," Rollo Hackett reminded Morgan. (Indeed you don't, thought Clarence.) "Now, let's see," he said, moving on to Clarence's cage. The chimpanzee and the pigeon regarded the head zookeeper nervously.

Hackett's face lit up suddenly, as if the words he was now reading were giving him special plea-sure. He turned to Morgan and smiled. "Look at this, Morgan," he said, pointing to the notebook.

"Your little buddy-boy here . . . excuse me, I mean your *son* . . . is going on a long trip. Better put lots of bananas in his suitcase."

Morgan swallowed hard. "What do you mean?" he asked Rollo Hackett. "I thought you said he was going to a zoo nearby."

"Well, he *was*," Hackett replied. "But things have changed somewhat. It seems that instead of going to a zoo in the next county, he'll be going to one in the next *country*."

"Wh . . . what?"

"Clarence here is off to London." Rollo Hackett turned to face the chimpanzee. "Cheerio, Clarence, ol' boy!" he said, and he moved on to the seal pool. Over his shoulder, he called out to Morgan, "Don't worry, he's not leaving right away. You won't have to get out your hanky till a week from tomorrow." He then muttered something to himself and stood, scratching his head, before the seals.

Morgan and Clarence looked at each other in dismay. So it had finally come to this; not only were they to be separated, but there was little hope they would ever see each other again. As for William, no hope at all was left. He might have been able to fly a few miles, perhaps even a few hundred, but he'd never be able to fly across an entire ocean.

"Come on, Morgan, snap out of it," Hackett was saying. "Get over here." Morgan joined his boss by the seal pool, where Hackett insisted he identify each seal in turn so that he could determine where they were to be sent. Some were going to Lincoln, Nebraska, some to Vancouver, one to Tulsa, Oklahoma, and the remainder to Greenville, South Carolina. Unfortunately, as Morgan called out each seal by name, Hackett just muttered to himself and made notes in his notebook. As a result, neither Basil nor any of the other seals knew to which city they'd be going.

At last, Morgan and Hackett stood before the lions' cage. Lancelot and Guenevere eyed the zookeepers anxiously. Clarence and William, putting aside for a moment their own plights, listened carefully to hear what Rollo Hackett would say. He flipped to a new page in the notebook and said to Morgan, "You know what I have written here?"

"No," replied Morgan. "What?"

Hackett showed him the page.

"But it's blank," Morgan said.

"You got it," said Rollo Hackett. "As blank as the fate of these two. One lion, one lioness, both over the hill. Nobody wants 'em, Morgan. You know what that means, don't you?"

Morgan averted his eyes from Lance's and Gwen's gaze. "I know what you said it means," he said in a low voice. "But there's still a chance, isn't there, that—"

"Oh, sure," replied Hackett. "There's always a chance. After all, anything can happen in this world, right, Morgan? But there's a better chance that nothing's gonna happen, in which case—"

"Yes, yes," Morgan said, stopping Hackett before he could say more, "I understand. Well, we'll just have to keep looking, that's all. Surely, somebody somewhere will want to take them in."

Morgan looked back dolefully at the animals as Rollo Hackett led him away to another part of the zoo.

For the longest time, no one could find the words to speak. Each was lost in his own dark thoughts, some turning unfamiliar names over and over in their minds—Kalamazoo, Rochester, London—hoping to conjure up images of their future homes. But with each turning, the names only remained a string of sounds, bereft of meaning. Others didn't even have names to ponder; when they looked into the future, they saw nothing . . . nothing at all.

"Never have I felt so lugubrious," Lucy moaned at last.

"I have no idea what that means," said Daisy, "but from the sound of it, I suspect I feel much the same."

"How can I be parted from my own flesh and blood?" Lucy went on. "We've never been apart, not for a moment. Why, she'll be lost without me. And I . . . well, I admit it, I'll be lost without her." Lucy reared back her head and trumpeted loudly. When Ginger joined her mother, the two elephants produced a sound that was part alarum, part lament.

For William, their piercing cries might have been his own heart's song. He had quite forgotten what he and Clarence had been discussing earlier; all that remained of that conversation was the numbing realization that it would undoubtedly be one of their last. Clarence, however, felt differently. He did not mention it to William just then, but for him their earlier conversation represented not hopelessness but the only hope left. He knew it wasn't much, but neither, he thought, was a scrap of wood. Yet, a scrap of wood could save a drowning man. Clarence was not sure how his "scrap of wood" would save the zoo, but he was determined to cling to it until he saw land.

THE NEXT MORNING, Allison and Andrew arrived at the zoo wearing new T-shirts and long faces. Ordinarily, they would have looked for Morgan right away. But today, they were in no hurry. What they had to tell Morgan could wait. Besides, they wanted to be alone with the animals. Just for a little while. To watch them. To talk to them. And, though they hadn't really said as much, at least not to each other, to say goodbye.

Allison had always had a special fondness for Daisy, Andrew for Basil, and so it was with these two animals the children lingered longest this gray and breezy Friday morning.

"Did you miss me yesterday?" Andrew asked the seal. "We didn't come, see, because we were with our dad." Basil, perched on his flippers at the edge of the pool, listened attentively to Andrew's every word. "Usually we don't see him in the middle of the week, but it was his birthday and he decided to take the day off and spend it with us. We went to the science museum and . . . oh, let me tell you about this movie we saw."

"My dad really makes me laugh," Allison was saying. She rocked back and forth on the railing before Daisy's cage as she spoke. The giraffe tilted her head slightly, the better to hear what Allison was telling her. "He's always saying silly things and thinking of fun stuff for us to do. After we had supper in this restaurant last night, we went back to his apartment to have cake and ice cream. And he made us wear these funny hats. I felt a little dumb at first, because Andrew and I don't wear hats like that anymore; but Daddy said we had to wear them or it wouldn't be a party. So we did it to make him happy. But then I kind of liked it. Anyway, we sure laughed a lot. You know, Daisy, sometimes I wish my mom could be more like my dad."

"So the boy makes the dog his pet, see, even though he's really a wild dog," Andrew was explaining. Basil was trying hard to remember the details of the story so he could tell it to the other seals later on. "But his grandfather says that one day he's going to have to let the dog return to the wild. And the boy knows that but he doesn't want to, because he loves him now, see. Did I tell you this was a real old movie, Basil? My dad took us to see it because it was his favorite when he was a kid. And he said since it was his birthday, we should go see what he wanted to see. Which was okay with me, 'cause I really liked it. Anyway . . ."

Allison wasn't looking at Daisy now. But she knew the giraffe was still listening. "My mom used to make him marble cake with chocolate frosting every year for his birthday because that's what he liked," she said. "I asked her if she'd make a cake for him this year, but she said she didn't think that was such a good idea. This cake he bought tasted like it was made of cardboard or something. I didn't even finish my piece." Allison stopped speaking for a minute, then said suddenly, "Oh, you know what we got him for his birthday, Daisy? A new tennis racket. Well, my mom gave us the money. But he was real excited. He said it was just what he wanted. Which we knew, of course. That's why we got it."

Andrew had finished describing the movie and was now telling Basil a joke he'd learned from his father. Basil barked appreciatively, and Andrew, almost despite himself, began to laugh. It was at this moment that Morgan appeared around the corner.

"Well, you're in a good mood today," he said when he heard Andrew laughing.

"Morgan," Allison cried, running to meet the zookeeper. "We have something to tell you. Our mother told us last night—"

Andrew joined them. "She spoke to her boss again," he said, "and—"

"And he said she could do the story," said Allison. "The only thing is—"

"Yeah," said Andrew, "the only thing is she has to do it the day the zoo is closing."

"That's next Tuesday," Morgan remarked. He smiled and shook his head a little sadly. "I'm afraid that will be too late to do us much good. After all, the animals are going to be . . ." He stopped himself in midsentence.

"The animals are going to be what?" asked Andrew.

Reluctantly, Morgan went on. "They're going to be shipped off to other zoos starting on Wednesday," he said. "So, you see, even being on television won't help us at this point."

Eyes wide, Andrew and Allison looked about at all the animals. "They're really going to be sent away?" Allison almost whispered.

"I'm afraid so," Morgan replied.

Allison began to cry. "I don't *want* them to

be sent away," she said. "I didn't think the zoo was really going to close. I thought . . . I thought we'd be able to save it."

"It *isn't* too late, Morgan," Andrew said suddenly. He was angry now, which, Allison knew, meant that he was on the verge of tears himself. "Okay," he went on, "so Mom has to do the story on the last day. So what? That doesn't mean we have to give up! We'll make our posters again and we'll get lots of people here and we'll put up a banner that says 'Save our Zoo,' and we'll *try*. Okay, Morgan? Okay?"

The zookeeper smiled again. "You're right," he said to Andrew. "We can't give up. We'll do everything we can, late as it is. Come on, let's go over to the office right now and start making posters."

"What about Mr. Hackett?" asked Allison, wiping her nose.

"Oh, he's gone off somewhere," Morgan replied. "He won't get in our way. Besides, what do we care about Rollo Hackett? If we feel like making some posters, we'll make some posters. Right?"

"Right!" cried Andrew.

"Right!" cried Allison.

"After all," Morgan said, "if we do save the zoo, it'll be no thanks to Rollo Hackett. And if we don't, what will he matter anyway? He won't be my boss anymore. I'll never have to listen to him again. And if there's one thing I'm tired of, it's listening to Rollo Hackett. Come on, Allison. Come on, Andrew. We've got important business to take care of. And if Mr. Hackett doesn't like it, too bad!"

"Yay, Morgan!" shouted the twins. And grabbing the zookeeper's hands, they ran off, laughing, in the direction of the office.

Clarence had listened intently to this entire conversation. He was very excited by what he had heard because it had given him an idea. "Television," he said to William. "That's *just* what we need."

"What do you mean?" asked William.

"You'll understand soon enough. Attention, everybody," he called out to the other animals, "I have a plan!"

"A plan?" asked Daisy.

"Oh, my," Gwen said, turning to her mate. "Lance, Clarence has a plan."

"A plant?" Lance growled. "What's a plant got to do with anything?"

"I knew you wouldn't let us down, Clarence, old boy," barked Basil.

"Oh, Clarence," cried Lucy. "Does this mean that Ginger and I won't have to be parted?"

"It may mean that," Clarence replied, nodding. "Yes, it may mean just that." He saw that all eyes were on him. "Now listen, everyone," he said. "Here's what we're going to do . . ."

11

Closing Day

IF NATURE WERE in perfect harmony with the emotions of man, the day would have been wrapped in a dapple-gray cloak, one that might, from time to time, be swept aside to reveal a bright yellow vest beneath. It was Tuesday, closing day of the Chelsea Park Zoo. And the hope that Morgan and the twins wore close to their hearts was veiled by a heavy cloth of melancholy. They wanted to believe that their last-minute efforts might yet save the zoo, but they were unable to shed the feeling that all, in the end, was lost.

Clarence and the other animals, closer to Nature perhaps, shared with her the radiant hopefulness of the sunny, cloudless day. They eagerly awaited the arrival of Nan Potter and her crew, for only after the cameras began to roll could they put into action Clarence's plan. It was true that they had all had their moments of doubt since Clarence had told them what he wanted them to do. After all, it was not a plan free from imperfections; one snag, and the whole thing could unravel. But they were determined to make it work. And never had they felt more determined than on this day when even the sidewalks sparkled.

A shadow crept slowly over the pavement, bedimming its glitter; six feet above, a red hat glowed in the morning sun. Both shadow and hat belonged to Rollo Hackett, come to bid the animals farewell. He said not a word, but, with arms crossed, stood before each cage and rocked back and forth on well-worn heels. He regarded the animals with dry eyes and a satisfied smile. His smile vanished, however, as he approached the seals' pool. For there, off to one side, was a huge banner that read: "SAVE OUR ZOO!"

"Morgan!" the head zookeeper shouted. It

was a wonder that he didn't simply tear the thing from where it hung.

"Yes, Mr. Hackett?" Morgan called from a distance. His voice, traveling at a faster clip than his feet, arrived before the rest of him. "Is something the matter?" he asked, turning the corner of Daisy's cage.

Hackett was shaking a finger at the twins' handiwork. "What is the meaning of this?" he demanded to know.

Morgan remained calm. He was not about to let Rollo Hackett bully him, not today. "It's for the news program, Mr. Hackett," he said.

"*What* news program!?" Hackett exploded.

"The news program about the closing of the zoo," Morgan said simply.

"But that was last week—"

"No," said Morgan. "It was supposed to be last week, but the television people never came. So they're coming today instead."

Rollo Hackett's face was fast approaching the color of his hat. "You never told me anything about this!" he yelled.

Ever so slightly, Morgan's lips turned up at the corners. "I don't tell you everything," he replied.

If such a thing were possible, smoke would have poured from every opening in Hackett's head. But before he could respond at all, there came a low rumble of footsteps and voices, which grew and grew until all at once the zoo was filled with people. Allison and Andrew ran through the crowd to Morgan's side.

"Morgan!" cried Andrew. "Look at all the people we got!"

"Did you do this?" Morgan asked.

Andrew said with a shrug, "Oh, it was no big thing."

"No big thing!?" said Allison. "We've just been standing outside the park for the last half-hour getting people to come in. One woman said to us, 'But the park isn't safe.' And do you know what Andrew said, Morgan? 'Don't worry, lady, I'll protect you from the pigeons.'"

Morgan had to laugh at that (William, who was nearby, chuckled, too . . . in a pigeon sort of way), but Rollo Hackett found nothing amusing. He snorted like an angry bull and stormed off.

"I don't think Mr. Hackett's very happy about this," Morgan said.

"I don't think Mr. Hackett's very happy, *period*," commented Andrew.

"True," Morgan agreed. "Very true."

"Maybe he'll be happier if we save the zoo," Allison said.

Morgan shook his head. "I don't think so," he replied. "I'm not sure what it would take to make Mr. Hackett a happy man, but I don't think saving the zoo would do it."

Clarence, who had been listening to this conversation, whispered to his friend, "Well, I guess *we* know what would make Rollo Hackett happy, don't we, William?"

William's head bobbed up and down. "Yes," he said, "and soon everyone else will, too. Oh, dear, Clarence, I'm afraid I'm getting a little nervous."

"Now, don't worry," the chimpanzee assured him, "everything will be fine."

"But I have such an important part to play. What if . . ."

"You must not ask 'what if', William!" Lucy declaimed from the next cage. " 'What if' is for the pigeonhe—Oh, I beg your pardon . . . I mean to say, the chickenheart—Oh, you know what I mean: the cowardly! We must be brave, William, if we are to succeed."

"Aren't you nervous at all?" William asked Lucy. "Even a little?"

"My dear," the grand elephant retorted,

"you forget that I am an artiste. This little charade I have been asked to perform today is a mere bubble on the histrionic champagne I have sipped in my time."

"Oh, Mother!" Ginger said.

"Besides," Lucy went on, speaking softly now, "if I don't believe we can succeed, with all my heart, then I am faced with the prospect of never seeing my daughter again. Now I ask you, William: what choice do I have? What choice do any of us have? We must be brave."

William did not have time to answer (though he was feeling much bolstered by Lucy's pep talk), because a sudden commotion drew his attention away.

"They're here!" he exclaimed. Nan Potter and two men, one carrying a camera, were weaving their way through the crowd, which fell back to make room for them. Some people whispered, "That's Nan Potter from the six o'clock news." "Yes, yes," cried others. "You know, she's even nicer-looking in person than she is on television." For others still, words could not express the sudden transformation the appearance of a celebrity and a television camera had made in their ordinary lives.

"Yes," said Clarence, "they're here. And that means it's almost time. Good luck, William."

William cooed, "Good luck to you, too, Clarence. Good luck to us all."

The twins, dragging Morgan by the hand, ran to greet their mother.

"This is Morgan," they called out.

Nan reached out her hand to the zookeeper. "Hello, Morgan," she said warmly. "I feel as though I know you already. The children never stop talking about you . . . and the animals, of course. You're all awfully important to them, you know."

Morgan smiled down at Allison and Andrew. "No more than they are to us," he said.

Nan Potter surveyed the area. "I think perhaps we should shoot this while I walk around," she said. "That way we can get a good look at the place and all the animals." She turned to her crew of two. "I'll start over here," she said, pointing to the seal pool. "Let's get the seals and that sign in the background. Then, I can move on to the chimpanzee's cage and the elephants. Sound all right, guys?"

"Fine with me," replied the man with the

camera. The other man nodded his head, as the two began to set up their equipment.

In a matter of minutes, they were ready to roll. Clarence and William, nearly breathless with excitement, were ready, too. They watched anxiously as Nan Potter assumed her position before the seal pool, took her microphone in hand and faced the camera. The twins stood on either side of Morgan, blending in with the crowd, which was giving its rapt attention to the goings-on. Morgan held his breath; this was his last hope, he believed. But, of course, he didn't know what the animals had in mind.

"Today is a sad day for our city," Nan Potter said in her cool, professional voice. "The Chelsea Park Zoo, which has delighted thousands of people for many years, is closing its gates."

"There aren't any gates," Andrew mumbled.

Allison shushed her brother. "It's just an expression," she said.

"Many people have gathered here today," Nan went on, "to say goodbye not just to the animals but, perhaps, to a way of life as well." She turned slightly and looked at the banner behind her. "Some people don't want the zoo to close. They are fighting to save it. But *can* it be saved? Perhaps. Perhaps if others care enough to join their fight." She began to move away now in the direction of Clarence's cage.

"This is it," Clarence squeezed out between tight lips. "All set, William? Lucy?"

"All set," the pigeon and the elephant answered as one. William moved through the bars of Clarence's cage and fluttered to the railing before it.

Clarence suddenly found himself the object of the television camera. "This is Clarence," Nan Potter was saying, as she glanced over her shoulder at the chimpanzee. "The zoo is his birthplace and his home. But soon he will be crated off to a new home, one far from—"

All at once, a terrifying screech shattered the air and brought Nan's words to an immediate halt. Everyone looked toward the cage next to Clarence's, for this is where the awful sound had come from. There, Lucy staggered about as if in a state of delirium. She tottered from one side of the cage to the other, bellowing wildly and nearly pinning her daughter to the wall in the process.

"All right," Ginger said in an aggravated whisper to her mother, "drop already."

With that, Lucy gave one final shriek and fell with a crash to the ground.

The crowd gasped.

"Something's wrong with Lucy!" Morgan cried in alarm. "She's sick. Out of my way, please, out of my way." The zookeeper pushed forward, removing his keys from his belt as he did so. This was William's cue.

"Keep the camera going," Nan Potter shouted. Then in her hushed newscaster voice, she said, "It appears that one of the elephants has just been stricken. The zookeeper is coming to the—"

But before she could finish her sentence, even before Morgan could reach Lucy's cage, William took flight. He swooped down and caught Morgan's keys in his beak.

Morgan was so taken by surprise, he didn't realize at first what had happened. But Nan Potter saw it all. "Hard as it is to believe, a pigeon has just grabbed the zookeeper's keys right out of his hands," she reported. "And now it appears . . . yes, he's turned them over to the chimpanzee."

As the camera recorded the amazing events, Clarence, keys in hand, rushed to his door and, reaching around, opened it quickly with the key he knew was his. He threw open the door, jumped down onto the pavement, bolted through the crowd and away.

"After him!" someone in the crowd cried out.

"Keep rolling!" Nan ordered her cameraman as they, along with everyone else, ran off in pursuit of the runaway chimp.

Morgan was in something of a daze at this point. He couldn't understand what had gotten into Clarence and William. And he was worried about Lucy.

"Clarence is trying to tell us something," Andrew told Morgan. "We've got to go after him."

"I always knew he was smart," Allison said. "Come on, Morgan. Hurry!"

"But what about Lucy?" Morgan asked.

"She's fine!" Andrew shouted, grabbing Morgan's hand. "Let's go!"

And, indeed, when Morgan looked back at the elephants' cage, there stood Lucy, chewing on some straw, as if nothing had happened at all.

By the time Morgan and the twins reached them, the crowd had followed Clarence to the Jungle Playland area of the zoo. There, the sudden uproar had so startled Rollo Hackett and his two companions that they had run off, leaving an upturned red hat and a tumble of playing cards. They didn't go far though; through his lens, the cameraman could make out three figures peering around the corner of a ramshackle refreshment stand.

"The chimp seems to know what he's doing," Nan said to the camera. "He's led us to another part of the zoo, one that looks as if it hasn't been in use for years. Now, he's . . . he's running to a trunk of some sort and . . ."

Clarence tugged at the lid of the old storage trunk near the children's zoo, succeeding after a moment's struggle in prying it open. "Now," he cried to William, who was hovering in the air above him, "the truth, at last! Let them all see for themselves!"

As Clarence threw back the lid, the crowd rushed forward. But William saw what was inside the trunk before they did. And he was stunned at the discovery.

"Rags!" he called out to his friend. "There's nothing but rags, Clarence."

Clarence's head jerked round to inspect the contents of the trunk. William was right! There were only rags where there should have been. . . . Perhaps underneath, he told himself. Frantically, he began tossing the rags out of the trunk. They flew higgledy-piggledy into the air, landing on the ground and, accompanied by whoops of surprise, on some of the people who were standing close by.

"What is the chimpanzee looking for?" Nan Potter asked the camera earnestly. "It appears he has led us to this trunk to show us something. Unless, of course, we are applying human logic to the aimless actions of an agitated ape." Pleased with herself by this last turn-of-phrase, Nan turned to see what was now happening.

Morgan had worked his way through the crowd and was kneeling by Clarence's side. Clarence paid him no attention at first. He just stood, staring in disbelief at the emptied trunk. Under the rags, he had found nothing but a family of mice, squealing now in protest at the angry whirl-wood that had disturbed their peace.

"How can this be!" he exclaimed. To the crowd, of course, his words sounded like gibber-ish, but to William they made perfect sense.

"I don't know," the pigeon replied, "unless we were wrong about—"

"We're not wrong," said Clarence emphatically. "I *know* we're not. Maybe they moved them. Maybe . . . maybe—"

Morgan looked with concern at the chittering chimpanzee. "What's wrong, Clarence?" he asked. "What are you trying to tell us?"

Clarence returned Morgan's bewildered gaze with one of his own. The rags he had just pulled from the trunk might as well have been a magician's scarves, for they had made his hopes vanish into thin air. Sadly, he reached out his hand to Morgan.

"Come on, my friend," said the zookeeper, taking Clarence's hand, "I think we'd better get you back to your cage. I just wish I knew what this was all about."

The twins had moved forward, and now joined Clarence and Morgan by the trunk. "Maybe he's upset about the zoo closing," Allison suggested.

"Yeah, he probably just wanted to get everybody's attention," said Andrew.

"Well, he certainly succeeded," a man nearby said. The crowd chuckled.

Just then, Rollo Hackett's shadow fell across the foursome. "What seems to be the problem?" he asked Morgan sternly.

"I don't know, Mr. Hackett," Morgan answered. "It's Clarence. He—"

Without waiting for Morgan to finish, Hackett turned and faced the crowd. "All right," he said. "The show's over. Everybody can go home now." Then, looking in the direction of Nan Potter, he called out, "And you, lady, the show's over for you, too. Tell that camera guy he's through takin' pictures."

Nan Potter eyed Hackett suspiciously. "All right," she called back. Then turning to her cameraman, she said softly, "Keep the camera running. There's something funny going on here, and I want to know what it is."

The crowd began to disperse. Morgan and Clarence, followed by the twins, moved slowly away from the trunk. It was as they were passing through the entranceway to the amusement area that the downhearted chimpanzee heard William say, "Well, we tried, Clarence. You can't say we didn't try."

"Where are you?" Clarence called out. "I don't see you."

William cooed. "I'm right above you," he said. "On the elephant."

The elephant? thought Clarence. He looked up and couldn't believe his eyes. There, in the middle of the sign that read "Jungle Playland", sat William, perched on the wooden elephant's . . . *trunk.*

"That's it!" Clarence cried.

Before the startled zookeeper knew what was happening, Clarence scrambled up onto his shoulders and from there took a giant leap to the elephant's head. William barely had time to get out of the way as Clarence grabbed hold of the trunk and swung back and forth, back and forth, until suddenly—

The crowd looked up. Morgan and the twins held tight to each other's hands. Nan Potter spoke rapidly into her microphone. "The chimp is hanging onto the elephant's trunk now," she said. "It seems that the trunk is loosening. I don't know what he's trying to do, but . . . wait a minute, it looks as if he's going to fall . . . he's about to—"

CRACK! The wood split apart, and Clarence, holding tight to a fragment of the trunk, fell to the ground amidst a glittering shower. Jewels of every color and no color at all, golden bracelets, diamond earrings, pearls and emeralds and rubies spilled in a steady stream from the elephant's head. The crowd rushed forward to scoop them up as if they were candies falling from a broken piñata.

Suddenly, a voice cried out, "Hey, that's ours!"

Heads spun round, as did the camera recording the events, to discover a tall, gangly man in the distance. One of his hands held what appeared to be a wig; the other wagged an outstretched finger. "Those are ours!" he kept shouting. "Ours!"

The two men on either side of him began punching him in the arm. "Shut up!" cried the man some recognized as Rollo Hackett. "Geez, Duffy," the other man said. "You picked a fine time to start talking! What's the matter with ya, anyway?"

"But they're ours," cried the tall man named Duffy. "They can't have them. They're ours!"

"Gee," said Andrew to no one in particular, "I'll bet those guys are the jewel thieves!"

But Morgan was listening, and he nodded his head slowly. "You're right," he told Andrew. "They must be the thieves. But that would mean Mr. Hackett . . ."

Other people heard what Morgan and Andrew were saying. "Thieves!" someone called out. "Thieves!" another echoed. And the word raced through the crowd as fingers were pointed and cries of "After them!" and "Don't let them get away!" were hurled in the direction of the three men.

All at once, the crowd began to move toward Rollo Hackett and his two companions. "Let's get out of here!" Hackett shouted. Setting off in the direction of the animals' cages, they quickly turned their fast-paced walk into a run as they looked back to see the crowd closing in on them. Duffy's wig fell from his hand and was soon trampled into the dirt.

Clarence, Morgan's keys still gripped tightly in his hand, rushed ahead of the crowd and almost caught up with the escaping criminals. But it was not his intention to catch them himself; no, he had something quite different in mind.

As the three men raced through the compound, Clarence jumped up onto the ledge of Lance's and Gwen's cage. Fumbling for the right key, he said breathlessly, "All right, you two, this is your big chance." Suddenly, a key slipped into the lock, turned, and the door swung open. Clarence, hanging on, swung with it, and cried out to the charging lions, "Go get 'em!"

Roaring ferociously, Lance and Gwen set off in pursuit of Rollo Hackett and his two cohorts. The sound, which seemed to startle its makers, brought a cheer from the other animals and a stunned silence from the crowd who came to a grinding halt when they realized two lions were on the loose.

Nan and her crew didn't miss a bit of the action. "Clarence, that incredible chimp, has released the lions from their cages," Nan said. Her words spilled out rapidly as she tried to keep up with what was happening. "And the lions are now chasing the three men attempting to escape. Wait, what's this? One of the men has turned around . . . he sees the lion . . . he—"

A scream of sheer terror erupted from Duffy's mouth. He stood frozen in his tracks as the two roaring lions came closer and closer. Hackett and the stocky man turned to pull Duffy along. It was then that . . .

"All three men see the lions now," reported Nan Potter. "They look as if they don't know what to do. Well, who would in their shoes? After all, it's not everyday one finds oneself being chased by lions! One of the men is pointing to a tree. I believe they're going to climb up . . . yes,

yes . . . that's what they're doing . . . they're climbing the tree."

Rollo Hackett clambered up the branches of the tree in such a hurry that he missed the irony of the moment. But it was not overlooked by the thousands of viewers who tuned in that evening to watch the most astonishing news story many of them had ever seen. For there on their television screens was the image of three men hanging from a tree, their ankles being nipped by the lions who had "captured" them, while suspended from the same tree was a huge banner bearing the words, "SAVE OUR ZOO!"

"The three men were led away by police some time later," Nan Potter informed her viewers. "After the strain of being held captive by snarling jungle beasts, their arrest apparently came as something of a relief. The men readily admitted that they were, in fact, the jewel thieves who have been plaguing our city. Rollo Hackett, head zookeeper of the Chelsea Park Zoo, confessed to being the 'brains' of the operation. The other two men, one of whom dressed as a woman in order to confuse witnesses, actually committed the robberies. The stolen jewels, gathered by the crowd who had come to the zoo today to bid it

farewell, were turned over to police and will eventually be returned to their rightful owners."

Nan paused as a new image appeared on the screen. In a little box over her left shoulder was a picture of Clarence and Morgan. "What makes this story so remarkable," the newscaster went on, "is the fact that it was the zoo's animals, seemingly under the leadership of this chimpanzee, who revealed the whereabouts of the stolen goods and made possible the capture of the criminals. When informed of today's incredible events, Mayor Thayer announced that the closing of the zoo will be postponed, while he and the City Council consider the proper course of action. It is his intention to call an emergency meeting of the Council to discuss the matter. One thing seems certain: the animals, who were scheduled to be shipped off to other zoos starting tomorrow, can rest easy tonight. The Chelsea Park Zoo is still their home and, if all goes well, it will remain just that for a long, long time to come."

Now, if you had been out for an early evening stroll, and you happened to be in the vicinity of the Chelsea Park Zoo just then, you would have been given quite a start by the racket these last words produced. If your curiosity were sufficiently aroused, you might have gone looking for the cause of such a commotion. And what you would have found, if your search were a successful one, was a scene almost as amazing as the others that had taken place at the zoo that day.

There, in the middle of a compound of cages, sat a television set, its tangle of extension cords trailing off into the distance. Before it were an old man and two children, laughing and cheering, and so full of joy they barely knew what to do with themselves. And on all sides, laughing and cheering in their own way, were the animals: trumpeting elephants, barking seals, a chittering chimpanzee, a cooing pigeon, and, making the grandest sound of all, a lion . . . a lion who, just that day, had remembered how to roar.

12

Morgan's Zoo

NAN POTTER'S BOSS was ecstatic. It may have been the animals who captured the thieves, but it was Nan who captured the biggest news story of the year. No sooner had she finished her report on the six o'clock news than the telephone at the station began to ring . . . and ring . . . and ring.

"What can we do to make sure the zoo stays open?" callers wanted to know. "We mustn't let those wonderful animals be sent away!" "Whose idea was it to close the zoo anyway? We never heard of such a thing!" "Would it help if we sent money?"

To all the questions, the answer was the same: "Call the Mayor's office. Let the Mayor know how you feel."

And so it was that the very next day, Mayor Thayer called a press conference, and Nan Potter found herself once again at the zoo.

By the time she arrived with her crew, a large crowd was already assembled in the midst of the animals' cages. Reporters and photographers, curiosity-seekers and well-wishers, all were milling about, snapping pictures of the zoo's famous residents and talking excitedly among themselves about the previous day's extraordinary events.

A sudden hush fell on the crowd as Mayor Thayer, laughing and shaking hands with those he passed, made his way to the area in front of Clarence's cage where a makeshift podium awaited him. Fast on his heels was a tiny woman whose dress and straw hat, covered as they were with flowers, might have suggested the serenity of a country garden were it not for the fact that she exuded such a busy air; she was, perhaps, the bee in her own bonnet.

Before the Mayor reached the podium, he stopped to speak with someone in the front of the crowd. From across the way, Nan Potter realized that the man he was talking to was none other than Morgan. His slicked-back hair and ill-fitting suit had sufficiently disguised him so that Nan had walked right by him only minutes before and recognized nothing but the strong aroma of mothballs. Suddenly, she felt a tug at her sleeve.

"Well, hello, you two," she said, looking down at Allison and Andrew. "I wondered where you were hiding." She smiled as she observed that the twins, like Morgan, had dressed up for the occasion.

As the Mayor began to speak, the animals moved forward in their cages. Basil, straining to see, expressed his desire for those blocking his view to get out of the way. But no one paid him any attention; no one, that is, except Lucy, who told him in no uncertain terms to stop barking so that she and the others could hear the Mayor.

"And so," Mayor Thayer was saying, "the Council has agreed that such an important zoo with such . . . such *unusual* animals *must* be kept open."

The crowd cheered.

"But *how?* you may ask," the Mayor went on.

"With all the financial problems of the city, with the park's reputation . . . undeserved as it is . . . for being unsafe, *how* do we intend to keep the zoo open?"

"*I*'ll tell you how," cried a voice that crackled like a Fourth-of-July sparkler. The tiny woman who had followed Mayor Thayer to the podium stepped forward.

"I was just getting to that," the Mayor said.

"Well, then get to it," the woman snapped. "My bunions are killing me."

The Mayor smiled. "Ladies and gentlemen, I'd like you to meet Mrs. Leticia Brickle. Mrs. Brickle, as you probably know, was one of the unfortunate victims of the jewel thieves. But, thanks to Clarence and the other animals here, everything that was stolen has been recovered. She called me this morning to say—"

Leticia Brickle yanked an envelope out of her purse and shoved it at the Mayor. "I want you to have this," she told him. "It's a check for a heck of a lot of money. I don't remember how much right now, but that's not the point. The important thing is that you use it to get this zoo in shape, fix up whatever needs fixing, spruce the joint up, put some cops in the park if that's what it takes to get people coming here again, and *then* . . . I'll see to it that the zoo *never* has to close."

The crowd went wild. At first, Mayor Thayer raised his hands in an attempt to restore order. But then, when he thought about how long it had been since he'd last heard the sounds of applause and cheering, he lowered his hands and just basked in the glory of the moment.

When at last everyone quieted down, the Mayor motioned to Morgan to come up to the podium. Morgan, unused to being in the public eye, nervously straightened the tie he had already straightened at least a hundred times that day. With downcast eyes, he moved to the podium and wished he'd remembered to polish his shoes.

Mayor Thayer placed a hand on Morgan's shoulder. "This man, more than any other," he said, "deserves our thanks. If the animals in this zoo are special, it is Morgan who has made them so. His caring, his dedication to his job, his efforts to make the zoo the best it can be have too long gone unrewarded. Morgan, it is with great pleasure that I hereby name you Head Zookeeper of the Chelsea Park Zoo."

Morgan barely heard the jubilant cries that erupted from the crowd or the soft whir of the television cameras closing in on him. Something much more important drew his attention, and that was the pride that radiated from the two young faces whose eyes met his. His gaze lingered there for a moment; then, as he turned to thank the Mayor, he found someone else beaming at him. Morgan broke into a huge grin and winked. Clarence winked back.

A short time later, as the crowd was drifting away and Nan Potter and her crew were packing up, Allison and Andrew ran to Morgan's side.

"Can we stay and help you feed the animals?" Andrew asked.

"After all," said Allison sensibly, "you're going to need lots of help now that you're the head zookeeper."

Morgan was all set to answer when he noticed the twins' mother watching them. There was a look about her eyes that made him pause. What was it? he wondered. And then he thought he knew. It was a sort of longing.

He placed his hands on the twins' shoulders and, moving in the direction of Nan Potter, he said, "You're right. I will need help. And I can't think of more able assistants than the two of you. But you're a little overdressed for feeding animals, don't you think?"

"We could go home and change," said Andrew.

"I have a better idea," Nan said, as she came forward to meet them. "Why don't you two come along to the station? You haven't been there in a long time. And I'll interview you on the show tonight. After all, you're an important part of this story, and it's about time people found that out. What do you say?"

"You mean we'll be on television?" Allison asked.

"Mm-hmm."

"All right!" cried Andrew. And then he thought to say, "Is it okay, Morgan? I mean . . . if we don't help you feed the animals tonight?"

Morgan nodded. "It'll be fine," he said. "There'll be plenty of time for that. You run along with your mother and have fun."

After the twins had said goodbye to Morgan and the animals, they took their mother's hands and walked along the path that led past the lions' cage, past the seals' pool, and out through the park. As Morgan watched them go, he heard

Nan Potter say, "And then we'll go wherever you want for dinner and—"

"Could we have Chinese food?" Andrew asked.

"Chinese food?"

"Yeah," said Andrew. "I've kind of gotten used to it."

Nan laughed. "All right," she said, "we'll stuff ourselves on Chinese food. And then we'll see a movie. And, you know, I was thinking that this weekend we could . . ."

Morgan could no longer make out their words; instead, he just listened to the sound of their footsteps growing softer and softer in the distance. And then, when that sound could be heard no more, another took its place. It was the cooing of a pigeon.

ON SUNDAY AFTERNOONS the zoo is bustling. Fathers with their sleeves rolled up and jackets draped over their arms buy brightly colored balloons from the balloon man, two for a dollar, and present them with the admonition to hold them tight to their wide-eyed children. Laughing mothers point out the antics of dancing elephants and ball-bouncing seals, a playful chimpanzee and a musical giraffe. The children dash ahead, leaving their parents calling out their names, anxious to see once again the gentle lions who, the story is told, leapt roaring from their cage to capture a gang of notorious jewel thieves.

For many families, for most families living nearby, a summer without frequent visits to Morgan's Zoo is as unthinkable as a summer without lemonade. And just as they are sad to have to leave when it grows dark, so the animals are sad to see them go. But everyone is comforted by the thought that there will be another visit soon. And then another.

And so on through each long and glorious summer.

A CAST OF CHARACTERS
TO DELIGHT THE HEARTS
OF READERS!

BUNNICULA   51094-4/$2.50
James and Deborah Howe, illustrated by Alan Daniel
The now-famous story of the vampire bunny, this ALA
Notable Book begins the light-hearted story of the small
rabbit the Monroe family find in a shoebox at a Dracula
film. He looks like any ordinary bunny to Harold the dog.
But Chester, a well-read and observant cat, is suspicious
of the newcomer, whose teeth strangely resemble
fangs...

HOWLIDAY INN   69294-5/$2.50
James Howe, illustrated by Lynn Munsinger
"Another hit for the author of BUNNICULA!"
                                    School Library Journal
The continued "tail" of Chester the cat and Harold the
dog as they spend their summer vacation at the foreboding Chateau Bow-Wow, a kennel run by a mad scientist!

THE CELERY STALKS AT MIDNIGHT   69054-3/$2.50
James Howe, illustrated by Leslie Morrill
Bunnicula is back and on the loose in this third hilarious
novel featuring Chester the cat, Harold the dog, and the
famous vampire bunny. This time Bunnicula is missing
from his cage, and Chester and Harold turn sleuth to find
him, and save the town from a stalk of bloodless celery!
"Expect surprises. Plenty of amusing things happen."
                                    The New York Times Book Review

AVON Camelot Paperbacks

**The beloved favorite
(with over 2 million copies in print)
and basis for the Walt Disney classic!**

THE HUNDRED AND ONE DALMATIANS

by Dodie Smith

The mean Cruella de Vil is dog-napping Dalmatian puppies all over the country and it's up to Pongo and Missus to rescue their own fifteen puppies. Fortunately, every dog in the country is ready to help!

"Seldom do we find a book which offers such total and sustained enjoyment . . . superb reading."
—*Library Journal*

"A tale overflowing with those prime requisites of a good story—warmth and humor, imagination and suspense—and a fascinating array of characters, animal and human."—*Chicago Tribune*

An Avon Camelot Book 00628-6 • $2.50